The Hidden Secret of the Andes.
The Apparition

Pilarica

The Hidden Secret of the Andes. The Apparition

First Edition: 2023

ISBN: 9781524318161

© of the text:
  Pilarica

© Layout, design and production of this edition: 2023 EBL

To our ancestors who have left us a wonderful legacy

Table of Contents

Introduction

Peru, land of utopias and abundance, has aroused passions of various kinds, from the most noble and self-sacrificing to the most abject and ignominious. Peru's wealth, real and imagined, longed for and exaggerated, inflamed European minds since the dawn of the sixteenth century. By dint of hardship, hope, ambition, creativity and scraps of lost paradises and Eden to be found, Europe was building the legend of Peru. This legend, combined with the news coming from the New World, gave rise to the first intelligible confirmation of Peru: destination and route of gold.

At that time, for example, it was said that the walls of the cities were covered with gold plates and that, in certain regions, after a storm, the rain would leave the gold nuggets on the ground that it had plucked from the Andean mountains. This is how the legend of abundance was followed by the idea of wealth, and this was followed by a jumble of associations, negotiations, pacts and acts that had as their main objective the appropriation of the prefigured riches. Driven by an urgent hunger for gold, and ready to challenge an almost unknown world, the men who arrived in Peru were confronted with barbarism and abomination not only with respect to the natives, but also among themselves. However, the greatest stumbling block on the road to gold was the Andes.

The Andes, mythical and mysterious mountains, represented a natural obstacle to the conquistador's tenacity to get rich suddenly. In his unfailing route towards uncertain treasures, the conqueror did not notice the true treasure already announced on the skin of the mountains: the spirituality of the Andean inhabitant. True opulence was not material, but spiritual. Despite all the ferocity of the conqueror and the systematic dispossession of the Andean people, an inalienable world composed of allegories, tales, fables, enigmas and customs will survive as majestic as those mountains and will be secretly transmitted from generation to generation.

The story you will read below owes much to the tireless desire of the Andean people to survive, and above all to their stubborn determination to preserve an identity closely linked to a land of embedded valleys, impetuous rivers and high peaks. The Andean landscape, rigorous and exotic at the same time, will be the spatial framework where the story of Helébora and her people will unfold.

Fortunata

In a remote and forgotten village in the Andes, located at an altitude of more than three thousand five hundred meters, surrounded by mountains and bordered by precipices, lives a young girl who, hindered by the actions of fate, lives in pitiful poverty.

Her name is Fortunata Rumi, a worthy descendant of a noble caste in ancient times. Throughout her life, Fortunata, a woman of dedication, effort and sacrifice, has preserved with great dignity the uses, customs, rites and ceremonies transmitted by her ancestors.

In her daily life, she worked with great care, always eager in what she undertakes; her house shines like a mirror, everything is clean and well ordered. Within the framework of honesty and respect for her fellow man, this shrewd woman of great courage often resorted to the best arguments to defend her interests.

However, in Cuchimilcos, which is the name of the village where Fortunata lives, once overflowing with riches, but today far from contact with civilization, the inhabitants live in a universe full of sadness and suffering. What afflicts them most is the cold and hostile nature of the surroundings and, above all, a primitive agriculture resulting from the infertile lands.

But one morning, out of her precarious condition, Fortunata, the last descendant of the Rumi clan, carries a terrible burden on her back and feels the urgent need to confide in someone who can offer her wise advice. Thus, without any hesitation, she leaves her home and descends the steep road. On the way he meets a passer-by whom he asks if the wise man keeps the door of his house open. Faced with such a demand, the man is paralyzed. Decidedly this woman has no brains, for she should know that the wise man of the village lives cloistered, never opens his door and much less talks to the inhabitants. Going and bothering him seems very risky given the wise man's bellicose temperament.

At first, Fortunata cannot get a single word out of the intern. It is only after taking a deep breath, looking at her with some disbelief, that he answers her:

"Woman, words are superfluous: your door is always closed."

And he quickly points with his finger to the house further down the slope, the one where a donkey is tied up at the entrance. Without adding more, the passer-by disappears.

The difficult route plagued with obstacles and the cold climate of the region forces Fortunata to redouble her caution. Despite the precautions taken by the young woman, a recent rainfall causes a landslide, dragging huge rocks that roll down the road to the village. What a terrible situation! It's every man for himself! Helpless, the young woman is immobilized in deep fear.

Suddenly, the feeling of being an orphan of life with no one to count on invades her, and at that precise moment her instinct cries out to her to keep her existence safe.

The stones continue to roll, and Fortunata is the only person in the village. In desperation, she speeds up her pace. Blinded by fear, she does not turn around for a single moment, not even to see the danger she is in. Fortunately, she manages to take shelter in one of those stretches made up of the region's straggly trees, far from the reach of the rocks.

Breathless, Fortunata wants to cross the street and knock on the wise man's door in search of shelter. Unfortunately, the stones break loose with a regulated cadence, discharging a deafening noise, rolling and rolling through the desolate streets of the village. In this desperate panorama, Fortunata decides to remain motionless, waiting for everything to return to normal.

"Will I reach my destination?" she asks herself very troubled.

No one could have withstood such stress, she was a hopeless case and felt on the verge of collapse. Distressed, Fortunata has the strong conviction that this ungrateful experience will leave its mark on her life.

It is only at dusk, when the threat subsides, that Fortunata, still under the effects of fear and numb from the cold, springs up like a spring. The young woman leaves in panic and hurries to knock vehemently at the wise man's door. Shaken by her recent experiences, she nervously prepares herself for what she has to tell him: a few ill-formed sentences that in a few minutes will be expelled from her lips.

Fortunata continues to knock insistently on the door, as a way of instilling courage in herself.

Uncomfortable with the noise, Don Gumersindo gets up from his chair and hurries to open the door. He had no idea that this encounter would mark his life for eternity. He recognized the woman, the one who lives in the last house in the region, the house with yellow flowers. Why did she come to bother him? What did she want?

The frail young woman in front of him blushingly asks for wise counsel:

"Good morning, sir. I, I...," she stammers to him. "I'm expecting a baby."

Don Gumersindo does not believe what he hears and for an instant he is speechless. After recovering his voice, with a grim look on his face and a frown, he replies:

"How dare you come to my house? Who are you? And... where is your husband?"

"My husband... Oh, yes. He died in a landslide. You are the village sage, so I-I need your advice. All I know is that I'm waiting for spring. I feel a little disoriented. If it's a girl, I've chosen the name Helébora. As for the rest, I am lost."

Don Gumersindo thinks that this woman who has taken so many risks to go to his house deserved at least to be heard. Leaving her on the threshold is very risky, so, with a wave of his hand, the wise man invites her to enter his house. Fortunata, a bit self-conscious, nods obediently. Seeing the anguish reflected on her face, Don Gumersindo curiously prepares himself to listen to her. He offers her a cup of mate to calm her down, and she nods her head slightly and obeys without a murmur.

The sage observes her for a moment and strikes up a conversation to break the ice:

"Well, tell me, what is your name?"

"Fortunata Rumi."

Suddenly, something perplexes him. Don Gumersindo remarks the young woman's necklace and, when he hears her name, shivers run through his body. A strange feeling takes hold of him. A curiosity that unsettles him, that incites him to go into the unknown and inclines him to investigate further. To his surprise, he realizes that it is the same image drawn on that ceramic vase found by a shepherd in one of the many caves of the Andes. A mask.

The wise man remembers very well that day when the shepherd, trembling and a little unhinged, knocked on the door of his house very insistently. When he opened the door, the man handed the wise man a vase that he was holding in his hands.

Not knowing what to do with the object, the shepherd went to meet him, according to him, to demystify its origin. The most disconcerting thing was that, when he rubbed it, the mask's eyes lit up. The frightened shepherd ardently wished for some detail, some meaning behind those moving eyes. In short, something that would clarify his understanding a little.

Its origin was undoubtedly from the time of the Incas. Smooth, like any other vase, worn and eaten away by the passing of the centuries, but when rubbed, the same change took place: the eyes lit up like an incandescent flame. With an absorbed gaze, Don Gumersindo observed the strange symbols that adorned the mask. They were not artistic designs, but rather a secret from remote times: of that he was convinced. This perception had gone unnoticed by the shepherd. However, the unsettling fear of facing a mystery haunted the poor man, forcing him to divest himself of the find.

Before leaving, the shepherd advised the sage to handle the vase carefully, so as not to get into serious trouble. Then he said goodbye with a handshake and unhesitatingly left the object for the sage to guard.

Don Gumersindo, seeing the pastor's disturbing reaction - and frightened by the imposing object he was taking possession of - hid the vase in the back of his library.

Not long after, don Gumersindo reconsidered the possibility of investigating what was inside the vase. Touching it, turning it over, rubbing it... a thousand times he tried to interpret the symbols it contained without obtaining conclusive results. For many days, Don Gumersindo stayed up all night long with the desire to find out its contents, but after much effort he gave up, banishing the vase back to the back of his library.

Now in front of Fortunata, Don Gumersindo stares at the necklace like a fool, convinced that he has wasted valuable time hiding the vase without even deciphering the message. He gets up dry and swears to himself that he would get rid of its contents right now. "No more hidden mystery," he repeats to himself determinedly.

Don Gumersindo is sure that it all makes sense. "Which one?". The burning desire to go after the unknown drives him to act. Suddenly, he heads for the other end of the house. Trembling, but with unnerving resolve, he removes books from his library with the purpose of emptying it completely, carefully handling his most precious legacy. He proceeds with the operation, extracting the volumes one by one, stacking them haphazardly, and then continues with the most recent ones, already tired, throwing them on the floor in an infernal cadence until they are completely removed. Absorbed in his task, he forgets the presence of the bewildered Fortunata. The poor woman opens her big eyes and follows the sage with her curious gaze in his smallest movements.

Suddenly, Don Gumersindo stops his choice on the most insignificant object in Fortunata's eyes. Hidden among the pile of books is the aforementioned vase. Old. Dirty. It has lost its prestige, even its original color. "Perhaps it was found wrapped in a pre-Incan mummy," thinks the young woman.

"I found it, I found it," Don Gumersindo concluded with satisfaction.

She shows that simple ceramic vase, without grace, grotesque, dusty and very old. On it you can clearly see the drawing of a mask, identical to the one that adorns the necklace that Fortunata wears around her neck.

Suddenly the wise man is overcome with anxiety and approaches the young woman.

"Do you see? It is the same design as the necklace around your neck. Pay close attention, this time I will try to interpret the images that border the mask and rest assured that today this vase will release its secret."

Don Gumersindo takes the vase in his hands, cleans the dust and invites Fortunata to sit down. At first contact, the mask's eyes light up as they did the first time, then he turns it over and sees that the designs have been painted by a person with little talent in the art of painting. With the passing of the centuries the images are barely perceptible.

"You know? I had it hidden in the back of the library for fear that it was part of a terrible secret. It was given to me a few years ago, and since that day I have not been able to decipher its contents."

"Leave the secret where it is," says Fortunata. "That's not why I came."

"No way, something tells me that all this concerns you."

The sage, eager to interpret the message, picks up a transparent emerald pebble and closely observes the images until he realizes that they come from an ancestral people that disappeared centuries ago. Absorbed, anxious to unravel its contents, he scrutinizes each image, each illustration, without success. After several hours of effort, discouragement sets in and he has to face the reality that he has set himself an impossible mission. Worried, he rubs the vase again, but this time the sealed lips open slightly with delicate movements in the form of a message. Fortunata, who remains silent at his side, worriedly asks him if it is really worth the trouble. Don Gumersindo insists.

"Let it go without saying: a mystery surrounds this ceramic vase, and I'm about to find out."

The wise man, endowed with a lively intelligence, remembering the faint movements of the vase's lips, using some of his books and observing each image, manages, with a little ingenuity, to put together and dissociate some words until he reconstitutes a sentence:

"Behind a glass wall and its golden-eyed gate, the flower that will free the Andes from the forces of evil will receive the life of Lady Fortune."

Everything is strange. However, Don Gumersindo clearly understands that it is a prophecy. "Yes, a prophecy and... what is the meaning of it?

His mind explores all the unimaginable clues, discarding one by one, without solving the enigma. Apparently, his vocation as a village sage is of no use to him. An inexplicable fear takes hold of him and he realizes that time is not on his side. Saddened, he anticipates a sad outcome. In his desperation, both his gaze and his mind jump from one object to another and end up landing on the young woman's necklace. He remains engrossed in observing it for a long time, now he understands clearly and, like an illumination, he understands and shares his discovery with enthusiasm.

"Yes! It's in this mysterious vase that I have in my hands and that has intrigued me so much. It's all there! Everything is explained! Fortunata, you carry the solution with you. Your necklace is made of crystal..., it's the wall! And it's adorned with a mask with golden eyes! That's the door with golden eyes!"

For Fortunata, what the wise man had just replied was foolish and she sensed that, if she remained there, she would soon embark on a whirlpool of irreversible events. Her only desire is to escape from this suffocating reality.

"What are you telling me? What you just said is nonsense!" Fortunata replies with an energetic tone, expressing her uneasiness. "Impossible!"

"Yes, I'm sure! And, lady, Fortuna is your name, isn't it? And you have told me that, if you have a daughter, you would choose the name of Helebora, which is the flower of prophecy."

Faced with this forceful argument, the young woman's breath caught in her throat. But that's not all, after a few moments of reflection, Don Gumersindo hurries to warn her.

"Fortunata, listen to me well: you are in great danger if you are pregnant."

"What danger? I don't understand anything!"

"I want you to know and remember forever: a secret, whatever it is, will be jealously guarded by its guards. What I have just unraveled in this vase is a secret hidden for centuries. Unfortunately, by revealing it, we have awakened the specters that have guarded it since ancient times. As you can imagine, they will not remain passive while waiting for new events; on the contrary, they will start a relentless hunt and their prey... will be you and your descendant! Now, listen to me well, if you wish to escape from this sad outcome that destiny has in store for you and your daughter, you will have to cloister yourself in your home."

"Why?" asks Fortunata, increasingly lost and on the verge of tears. "What is this whole story?"

"It is written: the moment the person concerned becomes aware of this secret, unknown forces will be activated and will prevent the birth of the last descendant."

"How am I going to do it? I need to go to the market at least once a day... and give birth alone! Impossible! It's too much to ask of a poor woman without resources."

Fortunata's eyes are flooded with tears. She has risked her life to turn to the village sage for simple advice, and now she finds herself entangled with an incomprehensible prophecy. The whole thing is beyond the limits of the imaginable, and Don Gumersindo, aware of the problem, adds:

"You must be very careful," the sage advised her, "I remind you that during the gestation period you will be obliged to feed on your own crops and animals."

"What are you saying? Surely I won't have enough food to subsist. Nothing grows properly here, it's a real death sentence," Fortunata whines.

"Providence will be your ally. Come, I will give you a goat to provide you with milk. Follow my advice and you will not regret it." As Don Gumersindo is the one who has revealed the truth to Fortunata, he fears for his life and, frightened at having intruded, he makes a clear and imperative request: "Now, run. Ah, I forgot the most important thing: when the sun goes down, close your door and windows tightly, because it is at that moment that the forces of evil will come to the house. If there is a knock at the door, don't open it for anyone."

Fortunata has the unpleasant feeling that the wise man wants to get rid of her. And she is not mistaken, since, after the last piece of advice, Don Gumersindo opens the door wide and points the way. She would have liked to talk a little more..., perhaps even say goodbye, but she is not allowed to do so. The time for dialogue is over, the danger is real and close.

With the terrible promise to follow his recommendations to the letter, terrified and with her face covered with tears, Fortunata leaves the house of the wise man of the village, holding a goat in one hand and a handful of seeds in the other, thus heading for a forced confinement.

"Surely the day I fell pregnant I was under a bad influence," she repeats to herself disconsolately. Such is now her sad reality: a total, forced confinement until her firstborn comes into the world. With uncommon ardor, Fortunata begins her new life.

Filled with courage, she prepares the crops, cleans the house, piles up small logs of wood for warmth, weaves a few pieces for the baby, and finishes her supplies of fine herbs to satisfy her needs for hot herbal teas. The days of confinement seem long and tedious to her. Often, in order to endure this suffocating isolation,

Fortunata dreams of a little solitary stroll in the neighborhood. But she wakes up abruptly with the promise that she will not even look out the window so as not to arouse suspicion. Fortunata remembers the sage's last words and, obedient to his designs, continues with her discreet and monotonous life.

Before going to sleep, he gets into the habit of slamming the door and windows shut, as the wise man advised him to do. Despite her precautions, one fine day there is a very insistent knock on her door. The noise is so terrible that Fortunata thinks they are going to break the door.

She does not dare to open it.

Filled with fear, she chooses to hide under the table, cover her ears and fix her eyes on the door while praying ardently for this ordeal to end.

The next day, the same scenario is repeated, and the following days; however, Fortunata does not open the door.

And so the months go by. She is the first to wonder how she has managed to endure such terrible suffering, especially with no one to help her.

After so many heartaches, what she longs for most finally happens. Her baby comes into the world and everything goes perfectly. She is a baby brimming with life, a beautiful baby girl. It is written in the firmament that Helébora will be her name, and if this mysterious prophecy is accurate, hope will be reborn in the Andes. Fortunata harbors doubts, for a strong premonition warns her that the future will be full of obstacles.

But Fortunata is a strong and passionate woman. She is ready to accept the terrible designs that life has imposed on her and her offspring. The evil as well as the good; the joys as well as the sorrows.

The Picha Fair

Every year, since her earliest childhood, Helébora Rumi has waited impatiently for the opening of the famous Picha Fair. The village of Picha, located in a high-risk seismic zone, is elevated three thousand five hundred meters above sea level and opens its doors for an unprecedented event. The fair is a unique event of its kind and is fervently awaited by entire communities.

The renown of Picha is thus intimately linked to its famous fair, where the best objects and artifacts of artists and artisans from distant regions are exhibited. The simplest objects are crafted with such grace and finesse that acquiring an object from the fair, no matter how small, is synonymous with good taste. The works of Picha are exhibited not only in the meetings of wealthy people, but also in some improvised shelf built for it in the homes of modest people.

The fame of the event is such that every year a new contingent of foreigners enters the arteries of the fair to be enraptured by the novelties and traditional products of the region. There are even those who scrutinize with a magnifying glass the minute details and the harmony of shapes of the objects on display. These people with strange accents and atypical gestures are another attraction of the fair. To them is added the band of saltimbanquis from Lima who, with their colorful and gridded attire, make their way through the crowds, repeating colonial-era announcements. The itinerant singers, of course there are also some, repeat old Aymara and Quechua tunes of the events of a world lost in time. Helébora listens to them without understanding while, as every year, the images of the fair run over her memory until they become indelible memories.

Throughout the year, Fortunata Rumi, Helébora's mother, patiently economizes the sum of money needed to take her daughter to the fair. For Helébora, attending the event is the most precious gift her mother can give her. The mother leads a hard life but placid in her austerity, she is a woman respectful of traditions and has educated Helébora in the same way.

The fair is part of their habits. Both, mother and daughter, feel a great joy when they walk through the shelves and the artificial avenues of the fair. That is the reason why, from the beginning to the closing of the event, they stay with an old friend of their mother's, just a few streets away from the fair. Fortunata cannot miss a single moment, the fair is a privileged reference point to transmit to Helébora part of the legacy and customs of her ancestors; teachable that, when it comes to nurture your own culture, no effort is spared, however demanding they may be.

Fortunata's modest economic condition is not an obstacle for her to choose, among the innumerable objects displayed along tables and shop windows, those that she will lovingly give to her daughter once the fair closes. Arrived home, Helébora runs to jealously guard her mother's presents in a rustic box that she herself has made with pieces of wood and whimsically decorated with ceramic waste. These precious objects, substitutes for toys and dolls, cling her to a past that is intuitive in its forms but elusive and mysterious at the same time. Not without a certain fascination, day or night, Helébora contemplates her gifts from Picha, eager to find distant and immemorial answers to her early and truncated questions.

This year, as in previous years, Helébora's heart overflows with joy as the fair approaches. With only minutes to go before the metal doors open, she glimpses over the heads of the first visitors and Helébora's joy is infected by the anxiety that prevails in the surrounding faces. Time has slowed its cadence, and the minutes are counted in hours. And in that time amplified by the wait, some talk about the ups and downs of the trip, the weather, the peculiarity of the local people, the flatness of the Andean land-scapes and the events of last year's fair. Meanwhile, Helébora and the silent visitors imagine the colors, materials, textures, shapes, designs and volumes of the new creations. She wonders what objects will be exhibited on the main avenue, what shelves will be chosen to stand in the front row, what artistic attractions they will have prepared, how many visitors there will be this year and who will win the fair's prize for the best artisan. Fortunata and her daughter are at the front of the line, and so they listen to the hurried orders that the fair organizers dictate to the artisans.

As the minutes pass, impatience becomes more and more noticeable. Although the scheduled time for the official opening of the fair has not arrived, a conglomerate of disjointed whistles advances from the back of the rows. In a split second, Fortunata and Helébora look at each other and exchange faint smiles, oblivious to the sonorous discontent.

Suddenly, from the middle of the rows, a row of foul language rises up, which cannot go unnoticed by those in charge of the fair. Behind the roll-up door, a voice repeated over the loudspeakers urges patience and calm. Stentorian cries erupt from various quarters in response to the loudspeakers' admonition. Fearing that the protests might be followed by unruly acts, Fortunata firmly grasps Helébora's hand, who, with childish indulgence, justifies to herself the string of whistles, whistles and shouts by saying that the commotion is understandable given the year-long wait that everyone has had to endure, especially her, back in the long loneliness of her short years.

Minutes later, the sound of locks being unlocked announces the imminent separation of metal and earth: the metal doors begin to curl up, gradually revealing the profiles and contents of the first kiosks. In the meantime, fanfare music blares from the loudspeakers and preliminary rehearsals are conducted on the microphone before use. When the shutters are fully raised, the loudspeakers fall silent and the president of the fair takes the microphone to say laconically:

"Welcome to the famous Picha Fair!"

"Hurray! Bravo! Hurray!" shout several voices.

In an orderly fashion, the lines empty and disperse along the fairgrounds. An icy breeze blows through the place, forcing the future passers-by to close themselves in their jackets, jackets and coats. Helébora clings to her mother's lap, walking in step with her. Despite the cold, the fair begins to buzz with activity. Singers and artists are strategically placed on different stages, eager to beat the freezing air with the flame of their talents.

The idea of exhibiting a product of her own hands at the fair seduced Helébora the day her mother first took her to discover that surprising constellation of avid faces, greedy gestures, restless looks and primal glee revolving around offers, counter-offers and bargaining outside the laws of economics. It was a wintry day, frost thinly covered the ichus, and leaves of valerian and huamanripas hung from some of the counters. A musty, musty smell emanated from the ground, while the sky was dropping its first drops of rain. A slow, unobliged and constipated rain, which suddenly turned into a downpour. Under that torrential rain of barely twenty minutes, Helébora attentively observed the stubborn determination of a vendor of stylized vicuñas in silver fiber. She was refusing to sell one of her vicuñas to an angry character who had put enough money on the counter to buy the whole lot. Soaked from head to toe, Helébora began to realize that the Picha Fair, before being a market, was a place of encounters not only between human beings, but also between them and the objects that were destined for them. The craftsman and the artist, vicars of impenetrable designs, knew to whom each object was to be sold. The price was an accessory, the main concern was to identify the person for whom the product was created from among all the applicants.

Every visitor was awaited by his object; every object kept the memory of its future owner. That is why one of the peculiarities of the fair was the disparity in the attribution of prices. Apparently, there was no detectable logic.

A clay statuette could be sold at exorbitant prices, while an emerald bracelet could be sold for a derisory sum. Dazzled by the scene, Helébora wanted to belong to the tribe of artisan-artists, but, above all, she wanted to exhibit her works at the Picha Fair and thus enjoy that privileged contact between the creator, his work and the pretender to possess it. Soaked and splashing mud on her flanks, Helébora ran full of enthusiasm to tell her mother that someday she too would exhibit her "things" at the Picha Fair, concluding her short premonition with the phrase that would haunt her for the rest of her days: "My heart wants it".

From that day on, the Picha Fair became embedded in Helébora's dreams. In one of them, flying over the streets of the fair, Helébora saw a wounded vicuña moaning over a mountain of trunks, suitcases and tulles. Cautiously and pretending not to cause the slightest discomfort, Helébora descended to get a closer look and, when she wanted to caress the vicuña, she shrunk her muscles and looking at it firmly said: "Touch me only if your heart wants it". After which, he spread his wings, took flight and lost himself in the clouds. Helébora wanted to follow her, but no matter how hard she tried, she could not get off the ground. She was on her sixteenth attempt when her mother, stroking her hair, offered her the sunlight and a pot of cooked quinoa.

In another dream she saw herself surrounded by artisan-artists, all of them looking at her from head to toe, examining her with a magnifying glass as if she were a freak. Helébora, between joyful and fearful of so much attention, only managed to rummage through her skirts and show the product of her hands: an object made from old, faded scraps of cotton, linen and broom fabrics. Before the artisan-artists could show any reaction, the object fell, spread out on the earth and shook it with a dry noise, raising a small dust around it. Helébora bent down, picked up her object and, once upright, noticed that they had all disappeared.

She was about to leave when a little girl with matted hair and a faint, tearful face, tugged at her skirt and said: "I want your doll". Helébora was ready to give it to her, but the doll fell again and neither Helébora nor the girl could pull it off the ground. Without noise or dust, the doll slowly but progressively sank into an earth that began to crack, creating a hole that deepened like a crater. Crouching down, Helébora and the girl desperately tried to intervene in the immersion, stretching their arms in vain attempts to extract the doll from the earth's maw. Helébora awoke with her left arm cramped and hanging off the side of the bed.

In some mysterious way, the fair had even embedded itself in Helébora's dreams; over the years — and a little determination —she would become one of the most important characters of the famous Picha Fair.

Reading and Writing

Helébora and her mother dedicate themselves to the menial tasks of domestic life. As soon as dawn breaks, both enter their own particular worlds. Fortunata makes the first sounds of the day: noises of pots and pans that are confused with the morning song of the goldfinches. Her mother prepares the inevitable breakfast of fried corn, boiled potatoes and pieces of goat cheese. Helébora, on her own, takes pleasure in observing her little garden of wild flowers and herbs while a vague and then intense smell of lemon verbena escapes through the window. From time to time, Helébora brushes aside the weeds and leaf litter that the wind whimsically deposits on the garden. Then, invariably, she surrenders to the following evidence: her garden is not the same, it has changed as the clouds in the sky are constantly changing. Between the scent of lemongrass and the shy fragrances of the wildflowers, Helébora becomes familiar with the dynamics of change. While Fortunata repeats herself in her traditions and resonances, Helébora prepares her future mutations.

Breakfast is followed by trips to the market and the daily learning of the art of bargaining. Fortunata, who believes that "the right price is the one that gives the least displeasure", negotiates all her purchases, no matter how small. Some sellers avoid her, others insult her, but most accept her and enter into her scheme. Usually, after the usual tug-of-war where each side freely exposes its best and worst arguments, the transaction is settled with a joke. In such circumstances, Fortunata gives free rein to her hidden expansive nature: she laughs and protests with equal intensity and one might even say that she is someone else. These few moments of exchange provide the mother with the necessary dose of sociability to endure her daily isolation.

Fortunata and Helébora live an hour and a half's walk from the nearest town, and almost two hours from the market. The route to the market is silent, Helébora respects her mother's silence and tries to imitate her light step when the road is uninteresting; if for some reason Helébora is delayed, she then runs to join her mother's cadence without uttering a word. The return trip is made at the same pace, despite the half-filled baskets of vegetables and tubers.

Around noon they are back home. From then on, Helébora has the rest of the day at her disposal; although she usually helps her mother with the small household chores.

There are times when she goes out to contemplate and consume nature, strolling along slopes and hillsides that lead her to springs and arbors. On the way, she makes a bouquet of flowers that she aspires with delectation. Her journeys always end in solitary and impassable places: a grotto, a field of sunflowers, a stream, the top of a hill, an old fallen log, a gigantic rock, and so on. Sometimes he spends hours and hours in the same place; he closes his eyes and automatically the images of the observed nature are projected in his pupils. He reviews what he has recently experienced in extraordinary sensations of color and form, which gives him the illusion of duplicating reality, especially when he sniffs the bouquet of flowers. When she returns home, after eating what her mother has cooked, Helébora goes to bed in a state of inner exhilaration.

One fine day, at the market, Helébora and her ten-year-old daughter cannot help but be amazed when she notices that a new vendor has placed cardboard on top of all the products he has arranged in piles. What amazes her is not the cartons themselves, but the inscriptions on them. What do these insect paw prints mean? Why doesn't the vendor do as the others do? What need does he have to crown his products with obscure inscriptions? Driven by curiosity, Helébora turns to the seller and asks him uninhibitedly:

"Do you sell insects?"

"No, why?" asks the questioner.

Without saying a word, Helébora points to each of the cards with her index finger. The salesman laughs and asks the girl:

"Can't you read?" She shakes her head. "Can someone explain to this girl what my signs say?" asks the vendor, turning to the interns and other merchants.

Getting no response, the seller concludes that Helébora is not an isolated case: no one in the market can read.

Helébora then asks:

"What is reading?"

"Read? To read..., to read... Well, to read is-is... to know. That's it! To know many many things."

At that moment, Fortunata, who has just paid the "fair price" for two hundred grams of olluco, intervenes saying:

"I've finished my shopping. Let's go, daughter!"

On the way home, Helébora mentally repeats the salesman's phrase: "To know many things. To know many things. To know many things...". In the middle of the way back, Helébora breaks the unspoken silence that unites them and says to her mother:

"I want to learn many things."

"Very good, very good," Fortunata repeats.

"I want to read," says Helébora dryly.

The mother does not respond; she remains hesitant without slowing down her pace. Helébora does not insist. After half an hour, Fortunata's face changes from calm to enthusiasm and she turns to her daughter with a benign smile.

"Don Gumersindo Caspi! He will teach you to read and also to write!"

The Wise Man
of the People

The stooped old man relaxes open book on the outskirts of his house. He shakes his head toward the door with a distressed gesture and becomes disheartened at the thought of getting up again and searching for the medicinal herbs he so desperately needs.

At times, the sadness of seeing his years go by without having anyone to talk to, to keep him company, worries him. Since the famous finding of the ceramic vase, an irrational fear has taken hold of him, to such an extent that he feels afraid of being seen, caught with an object that does not belong to him. "And who was its owner?" he asked himself a thousand times without finding an answer. Don Gumersindo Caspi had lost track of time and sometimes wondered when his real confinement had begun. That confinement that he had imposed on himself after realizing that that Inca ceramic vase contained the existence of a transcendental message.

Resigned to his emptiness, he bitterly recalls the hard years of isolation. Only daylight prowls his house and it is enough for him to observe the outskirts of his home to realize that the gloom of night floods the road. Another day is over.

By then, distant from the problems of the village, Don Gumersindo Caspi shows up very sporadically. Sometimes he leaves his home, basket in hand, with the purpose of buying products that he does not grow in his garden. And other times, deluded, he plants himself in the corner bodega offering almost insanely much money to buy the magazines, books or newspapers that pass through town. The answer is always blunt: "We don't compromise with that kind of merchandise in Cuchimilcos".[1] He leaves and weaves his way through the steep and dangerous streets that lead him back to his home.

Fortunata knows that Don Gumersindo Caspi is the only literate human being in the region. So, once lunch is over, she takes Helébora to meet her future tutor.

They find him sitting on the sidewalk in front of his house sipping a warm coca tea. The encounter is expeditious and revealing. Fortunata, with the same aplomb with which she usually haggles over prices, prepares to ask Don Gumersindo to be Helébora's teacher of first letters in exchange for domestic work that the girl will do for the duration of the apprenticeship.

"Don Gumersindo, I am Fortunata, do you remember me? I came to see you a few years ago... This is my daughter, Helébora," she said, encouraging her little girl to cross the threshold. "She needs to learn to read and write, and... I thought you could be her teacher. Helébora is a docile child, she will learn easily. Her daily activities will not be disturbed because we will accommodate her

---

[1] Ceramic figure, made by the Chancay people, composed of atrophied arms and hands that were transformed into wings, with a touch of a crescent moon ending in a hollow where feathers were added. The general anatomy was human with little marked sexual characters.

schedule. In exchange, Helébora will clean your house and do some housework," Fortunata concludes.

Don Gumersindo thinks he is going crazy, nothing justifies such impudence.

"How dare they?" Don Gumersindo mumbled, recognizing the mother.

Her presence forces him to stir up a past he would have liked to bury forever. The sage remembers perfectly well the last warning given to Fortunata: "If you wish to keep yourself and your descendants alive, go into hiding and, above all, never come to see me again".

The fact is that the advice was useless. Indignant at such insistence and without speaking to her, Don Gumersindo swings between anger and uneasiness, and watches the faces of the two women out of the corner of his eye. He emphasizes the mother's confused intention to leave her daughter. It is indeed the same woman who years ago had deciphered the enigmatic prophecy of the Andes. The one that caused her so much dread.

Don Gumersindo, impassive, drinks his tea without even looking at them and does not say a word to them during the entire meeting. A lover of reading, he has a small collection of books that he rereads with some frequency. The old man was, book in hand, engrossed in reading a historical event when Fortunata and Helébora approached him. He has neither ears nor eyes for anyone.

The historical episode deals with the rebellion of the Chachapoyas and the magnanimity of the Inca from the *Royal Commentaries of the Incas*, by the Inca Garcilaso de la Vega. It keeps him absorbed. Immersed in his thoughts and in the light vapor of the coca, Gumersindo Caspi does not even notice the departure of the two women.

Anxious to convince the village hermit to take her daughter under his tutelage, Fortunata ignores the inclement weather. Sorrowful, after having spent more than an hour insisting on the wise man, they set out on the dangerous, unpopulated road that leads them home. Helébora senses that the task of convincing Don Gumersindo will not be easy. Both are crestfallen, and the journey becomes tedious and gray. To Fortunata the route seems endless, and a faint feeling of uselessness begins to invade her. At home, aching, and with her feet and hands numb from the piercing cold of the Andean sunset, she asks her daughter to heat water to drink a hot camomile tea. Rubbing her hands around the cup, Fortunata looks at Helébora's face and concludes:

"At least we tried, my daughter. Let fate take care of the rest."

Moments of discouragement are not lacking, but Helébora knows of only one weapon to break her future instructor: insistence.

Busy, she prepares to leave the house very early in the morning. She plucks some yellow flowers from her garden to make a bouquet and sets off, but not before asking her mother's blessing. Hurrying up, she approaches Don Gumersindo's house and notices that the man is watching her from the window. Helébora quickens her pace.

"Don Gumersindo!" he shouts in the middle of the street, "Don Gumersindo! Please open the door. I have a present for you."

Her sadness is great as she notices the man frowning as he closes the curtains and moves away from the window. The lack of response prompts her to redouble her efforts. After a few sterile hours of seeing that her attempts are fruitless, Helébora and her tender age find it very difficult to understand this attitude. Why doesn't Don Gumersindo open the door?

Helébora hears the arrhythmic sound of quiet but firm footsteps. Knowing she has been heard, she insists:

"I know it's inside. Don't make him beg. Open up, please!" Emboldened by the contempt, Helébora instantly opts for another tactic. I will not move from here until you have heard me out. I have a proposition to make. Please open the door. I know you are at home. Please, Don Gumersindo, take pity on me and don't leave me shivering in the street.

Gumersindo's life has dried up over the years and no human action brings him joy. The girl is insistent, but he lacks the courage to receive her. He just waits for her to leave.

The dry cold of the early evening forces Helébora to retreat. Her forced guard has not lasted long. The girl asks for little and the wait is long and useless. Faced with the man's indifference and the cold that penetrates her to the bone, Helébora leaves the flowers she had picked before leaving the house at the door.

This first unpleasant experience, far from discouraging her, drives her to continue. "He who follows follows gets it," her mother tells her one morning to encourage her as she gets ready to stand in front of Don Gumersindo's door, as she does every day now. Weeks go by, but the door does not open and not even a word comes back to Helébora. Almost overwhelmed by the futility of her efforts, Helébora, after six weeks of waiting and watching, decides to abandon the enterprise.

But one fine day, destiny, the architect of radical changes in the lives of men, approaches her. Helébora, far from imagining what she is about to experience, is guided by a strange hunch. Tired of waiting for her mother to finish her chores to go to the market, Helébora proposes to go alone and bring what she needs.

"I need to stand on my own two feet, Mom, and I have to start early."

Adopting a gesture of disapproval, Fortunata wants to curb her daughter's impulses. Suddenly, she understands Helébora's request. For the first time after her birth, she is confronted with the inevitable: the arrival and departure of children. Fortunata contemplates her before that decisive moment of her life and her request resounds as if she had just finished her sentence. Letting go of her daughter is painful, but it is better to do it little by little and it is better to start early. Finally, she lets herself be convinced. Helébora thus embarks on her initiatory journey, a journey that will take her away from childhood and bring her closer to adulthood, a journey that, she senses, will decrease her dependence and increase her autonomy.

Full of joy, Helébora sets off for the market without that familiar voice that warns her of the dangers of the route. Walking cautiously before the steep descent that leads her to her destination. When she makes it, Helébora thanks God for his presence. After an hour's walk, the girl finds a surprise: the gray donkey that is normally tied with a stake at Don Gumersindo's house is now, free of mishaps and impediments, wandering through the muddy wasteland.

"Maybe he's lost," says the girl.

A few meters away, its owner lies inert, buried in the mud and contrite with pain. The fall had been abrupt, Helebora judged by the state of the sage's torn clothes. Filled with horror, she looked around to find some charitable soul who could help her. In desperation, Helébora tries to find a way to help him, but finds only a few trunks of bark gummed with mud.

"There must be another way," Helébora repeated in anguish.

Frightened, she just runs and runs. Maybe she wants to go home and ask her mother for help. Or meet an unexpected passerby who will help her to help. Or, who knows, to come across a sudden apparition that will guide her. On her run, Helébora trips over a thick concave log and falls flat on her face but is uninjured. Only a few scrapes on her arms that she brushes off as she gets up and shakes herself. Back at the scene of the accident, he pushes the sage, trying to lift him up and place him on the donkey's back. After a great effort he is finally able to get him to his feet. Still in pain from the severe beating, Don Gumersindo loses his balance and under the effect of the pain he observes the horizon and pronounces:

"What a wonder! At death's door, two angels come to visit me."

Staggering, he stumbles over Helébora's foot and falls back into the mud. Under this act, don Gumersindo loses consciousness. Desperate to see the man relapse again, Helébora wades into the mud and uses her two hands to reach the pieces of logs floating in the mud. With each step, the greenish pool gets deeper and Helébora barely floats. Faced with the absurdity of her attempt, Helébora sees no alternative but to give up.

"I have to get out of this stinking puddle. I need help."

Despite her good intentions, without the strength and energy of an adult, it is impossible for her to assist Don Gumersindo. The girl's cries for help are heartbreaking when, not far away, on the hill in front of her, she sees the stretched silhouette of a human being. Hurriedly, Helébora runs with all her strength and, waving her arms, exclaims: "Help! Help!". Her voice prolonged by the echo of the mountains reaches the ears of the passer-by, who mechanically tilts his head and perceives Helébora's lanky physiognomy. Before such a revelation, the man descends the mountains in an almost irrational way. Helébora is impressed by the agility of her savior as he crosses the cornfields.

The sun begins to project its first rays on the shoulders of that providential man who in his hurried descent seems to shake the hill. In those moments, Helébora remembers those legends that her mother used to tell her about the ancient times.

"The mountain men exist," he mutters between his teeth. Here is living proof."

He is a god, there is no doubt about it. That man descends with giant steps, his footsteps are firm and thunderous to such an extent that the earth trembles with each of his movements. The powerful man reaches her side, ready to help her. Her first concerns go unanswered, for Helébora, still stupefied, remains motionless without uttering a word.

"Wake up, child, and answer me: what happened here?"

Helébora hesitantly stared at the man and, with a wave of her hand, pointed to the wounded man. In the blink of an eye, the mountain man has managed to lift Don Gumersindo's body onto the donkey.

"This man is in a very bad position," says the man on the hill, "we have to find a way to heal him. Do you know where we can take him?

Suddenly, it occurs to Helébora that the best option is to take him to the healer's house. The girl has heard many terrifying stories about this character, many sobbing children cry out to their parents never to take them there. In her case, Helébora has never suffered any relapse, until now she has enjoyed perfect health and her mother's care is enough to maintain it. However, the burning desire to meet her in person gnaws at her soul. Helébora needs to know what her secrets were, the working tools she uses with the children, her recipes and syrups. Taking advantage of the opportunity, and full of curiosity, she suggests to the man from the mountains to take don Gumersindo to the house of Tokapi, the healer. During the trip, Helébora does not exchange a single word with the mountain man, because, engrossed in her thoughts, she does not see the moment when she will find herself in front of the much feared healer of the village.

Upon arriving at Tokapi's house, the man from the mountains places Don Gumersindo on a bench. Before he leaves, Helébora approaches the giant as she tries to utter a sentence she has prepared. But he anticipates her.

"You are a brave girl," he says, stroking her head with an affectionate gesture.

Helébora thanks the man who came down from the hill for his kindness and slams the door of the healer's house. Inside, Helébora faces her dreaded reality: the woman stands before her. Silent and wrapped in a dark poncho, her haggard face reveals no emotion, her stern gaze seems to dig deep into the girl's soul. Helébora, completely paralyzed, wonders if after surviving the incident in the mud she will now succumb to this witch's spells. Only one thought crosses her mind: run away!

His eyes are fixed on the door; unfortunately, his legs do not obey him due to the chilling contact with the healer. He has no doubt, in a short time his little body will be transformed into a toad, a raven or perhaps petrified. He will never see his family again.

"Oh! Mom! Mom! Why did I disobey you?"

In front of the healer, Helébora is immobilized by the fear of being bewitched. Tokapi turns the wounded man over and rushes off to prepare some warm compresses. With a cloth smeared with an ointment of her own making, Tokapi covers his forehead while she examines the wounded man's condition.

"This smelly man needs a bath urgently."

Helébora breaks down in tears. She can't take it anymore. Her fear is reflected in her face. Tokapi approaches the girl and, caressing her tenderly, says to her:

"I understand that the inhabitants of Cuchimilcos believe that I am a witch and that I can cause harm whenever I want. Don't hurry, it's a false image of me. I'm going to ask you to go home to see your mother, who must be worried about your disappearance. Later, you can return with her and whoever you want to visit this poor man."

Helébora feels more secure when she appears in front of her mother, even though her hair is still stiff. Fortunata takes her in her arms and covers her with kisses. After examining her from head to toe, she undresses her to give her a bath. She spreads a cream that she herself has prepared from cereals and citrus fruits, and her skin and hair regain their usual appearance.

Sheltering her in a hand-woven cloak, she leads her child to the table, anxious to know why she is late. Around a cup of hot tisane and some bread, Helébora opens the conversation, recounting what happened. After several hours, trust is restored, and Fortunata is proud of her daughter.

From that moment on, the two stay at the healer's house for as long as the hermit of Cuchimilcos needs to recover. Don Gumersindo stays three days at Tokapi's house, and during that time he develops the conviction that something extraordinary is happening in his life. Despite his aching body, the love that the three women lavish on him knows no bounds. After three days of convalescence, Don Gumersindo is given the go-ahead to return home, accompanied by Helébora and Fortunata, with a bouquet of yellow flowers and an ointment.

"Don't forget, Don Gumersindo," Tokapi reminds him: "One application per day for thirty consecutive days."

At the threshold of the door, a beaming Don Gumersindo does not know how to thank so many cares and attentions except by stretching out his hand to Tokapi with a smile on his lips.

"You have nothing to thank me for," the healer replied. My task is to take care of everyone who needs my care. Besides, the one you have to thank is this girl, who brought you here with the help of another man.

Heading for home, Don Gumersindo departs with his two companions under a sky covered with clouds. The people of Cuchimilcos welcome him like a son.

"Times have changed," said Don Gumersindo with some bewilderment.

"No, Don Gumersindo," Fortunata intervenes, "There is none so blind as he who does not want to see. The people of Cuchimilcos have always opened their arms to you and, meanwhile, you have lived all these years closed in on yourself, dominated by your fears. Now life is giving you a new opportunity, do not waste it.

In the twilight of his life, fate seems to show a new facet, a more tender and welcoming one that will cause a radical change in his misanthropic existence.

Over time, don Gumersindo will open up completely to the tender and innocent girl that is Helébora. Between household chores, discussions and learning, his affection for the girl grows day by day. Always smiling, with an affectionate gesture, Helébora has come to conquer the heart of the misanthrope.

Helébora thus becomes his ray of light. She is the girl who fills him with love and attention, thus, little by little, conquering the heart of the village hermit.

The Decision

The friendship with don Gumersindo has radically modified Helébora's behavior; her new attitude surprises even the most incredulous. Used to take out and keep daily the souvenirs that her mother had bought for her at each fair to contemplate them with a singular tenderness and touch them delicately with her hands, Helébora showed a deep affection and respect towards her ancestors. Nowadays her interests are different and, oblivious to the cult of her ancestors, Helébora hides them under her bed. Fortunata, puzzled, does not understand the reason for this gradual change.

Her new occupations absorb her to such an extent that, obsessed, Helébora has the sensation of being possessed. As the months go by, the need to see Don Gumersindo increases. Not a single afternoon passes without Helébora visiting him. She devours the streets that separate her from her mentor, often rag in hand, ready to begin her household chores. When she arrives, a radiant smile covers her face. Immediately, she runs to ask him, to beg him, to read a new story together. There are many occasions when, concentrating on Don Gumersindo's stories, Helébora is transported to distant countries; on other occasions, without understanding exactly where she is going, she feels as if she were swimming in darkness.

Learning to read and write surprises her so much that, without realizing it, she learns by leaps and bounds. The stories collected by don Gumersindo contribute greatly to her inner growth. The confidence and security she has developed in such a short time lead her to believe that everything is possible if one really accepts the dictates of the heart, as the winged vicuña in her dream reminds her. Suddenly, with the clarity of lightning, an idea assaults her mind.

"What if this year I sign up to participate in the Picha Fair?" Helébora murmurs. Then she shakes her head, "No! It's foolish to think about it... Competing with the master craftsmen is inconceivable, they will find me presumptuous."

But no one would be surprised by Helébora Rumi's decision. At sixteen years old, the prospect of participating intimidates her; however, as time goes by, the desire gains weight. She remembers as if it were yesterday that special day at the Picha Fair where she carefully observed a stylized vicuña vendor, without articulating a word. He looked at her as if she were an illusion. Like a true idiot, she tried to understand the transactions that circulated on that shelf. And so it was, amidst her concerns and curiosity, when a strange call appealed to her heart, telling her — or perhaps demanding her — to take that course.

"Look inside yourself," a mysterious voice repeats.

"Who is talking to me? I don't see anyone nearby."

That message is wonderful, and that sweet and tender voice intrigues her in an inexplicable way. What happens next, many would call ridiculous. It is an announcement, a call that Helébora is ready to receive. Dazed, she rushes into her mother's arms and demands an explanation for what she has just experienced.

"If you really want to participate in the fair, you will be able to do so, but only if your heart asks you to. Immerse yourself in its depths, it is there that you will find the necessary forces that will push you to go beyond what you imagine. The source of inspiration awaits you, my daughter."

That idea deserves extreme care, Helébora cannot abandon it in the corner of the impossible. The curious thing is that Helébora feels compelled to investigate her ancestral cultures. The image of creation is not clear, but the almost insane desire bursts inside her.

This year, after the closing of the Picha Fair, the two women return home; Fortunata exhausted by the long days of walking among the kiosks and Helébora saddened by the challenge and invaded by that stubborn and vehement idea of participating in the fair. As twilight falls, Helébora continues to be dissatisfied for not having possessed an accurate image of what she can offer. Looking back to a past she has not been an eyewitness to leaves her naked. In her bewilderment, she wonders aloud:

"What toys did children have in ancient times? It is certain that they did not have those of today. But... what were their favorite toys? -Suddenly an image flashes into his mind. Dolls! Clearly they played with dolls."

From that moment on, she has the impression that she is on the right track. Helébora has already selected the product with which she will present herself at the fair, and this discovery delights her. The joyful expression brings out the jovial character that characterizes her. She knows for sure what she wants to exhibit, but she needs to know the type of dolls that were made in ancient times.

Early the next morning, Helébora announces herself to her tutor. She has a new illusion, but she must understand the importance of it. Moved by those bright eyes, those blushing cheeks and that face full of impatience, Don Gumersindo invites her to enter his room, suggesting her to tear out of her heart what is troubling her so much. Eager and enthusiastic, Helébora shares her interest with him.

"Don Gumersindo, I have come to see you because I have a great concern."

"What's the matter, Helébora?"

"Every year, my mother and I religiously attend the Picha Fair."

"Yes, I know that."

"Next year I would like to participate."

"It's not a bad idea. What are you going to present? Remember that you will be competing against very experienced craftsmen."

"That's precisely what frightens me," the young girl confesses. I would like to present dolls, dolls that at the same time serve as a connecting thread between our present lives and our past. Do you know of a town that has disappeared and is renowned for its doll making?"

"Wait a little while. Let me think about it, daughter," asks the wise man. If I remember correctly, there was a village in time immemorial where dolls occupied an essential place in the lives of its inhabitants. What do you think if we look for more information in my books?"

Helébora knows she has the unconditional support of don Gumersindo.

"Let's divide the work."

Overcome by the desire to participate, Helébora takes the search very seriously. Seeing the young girl's interest, Don Gumersindo gets attached to his encyclopedias, knowing for certain that he will find some clue there. With redoubled obstinacy, Helébora picks up by chance a book about sacred objects of ancient times. Showing it to her tutor, the latter reviews the chapter on sacred dolls.

"The only dolls that are claimed to have magical and protective powers are the Chancay dolls. Their renown was such that even little princes owned one. Is this what you are looking for?"

"That's right, Don Gumersindo."

"What a joy that my books have been useful to you. Unfortunately, we don't have a single image to inspire you. But don't despair, Helébora, it's only the beginning. The rest will come from your creativity."

"Yes, Don Gumersindo. You are right. Well, it's getting late and I should be getting home. I'll talk to my mother about it. Thank you very much for your help."

"And remember, daughter: those dolls were endowed with magical powers."

Helébora leaves Don Gumersindo's house to walk through those cracked streets that lead to her home. In spite of the penetrating cold of the region, Helébora walks slowly, counting her steps and thus preventing the dust from rising. Besides feeling joyful at the discovery, a deep sadness overwhelms her, as if inside she is certain that the idea of participating in the fair is far-fetched.

Silent, she arrives home and, with nothing more to say to her mother, sits in a chair to meditate for a long time. Fortunata becomes restless when she sees her daughter's state of mind and asks her a thousand and one questions.

"With don Gumersindo we discovered that only the Chancay dolls had magical powers, but I don't know any more, mom. I haven't even been able to see an image to inspire me."

"Inspiration will come to you later, daughter. Have faith and don't give up."

That night Helébora can't sleep and, in a somber mood, wonders why this selection was made. Since the founding of the fair, no one, absolutely no one, has furnished her shelf with dolls. "What kind of dresses to make for them, how to make them, what material to use? And, above all, how to explain their origins, virtues and charms?" she wonders. The task is arduous and her knowledge scarce.

She thoughtfully went to her room, repeatedly uttering the phrase "Chancay doll" without imagining that, in this way, she would soon glimpse a supernatural revelation. As she finishes her sentences, a strange sensation comes over her. Those words are lost in an atmosphere full of uncertainty and anguish. But a hidden secret is about to come to light. The words spoken by Helébora are enveloped in a disturbing, almost deranged air, and a mysterious halo leads them, slipping through the door and windows of the house, to set off in distant directions.

A miracle is imminent. After many centuries, thousands of souls imprisoned by the evil and vices of men have united their destinies in a common tragedy. A sign linked to the dolls. The supernatural revelation buzzes in the diaphanous ears of the spirits, who, hand in hand with each other, particularly protected in the Inca huaca, slowly move their light little bodies.

The discreet community of Pacha Rurac awakens from a long sleep.

In very remote times, they had made up the twenty-five thousand inhabitants who, after a fatal set of circumstances, saw their lives come to an end. Before that hecatomb, an unscrupulous being took possession of Pacha Rurac, the terrible anaconda.[2] And now, without knowing it, by mentioning the words "Chancay doll", Helébora has resurrected an entire people condemned to oblivion whose awakening heralds a new era.

---

[2]   "In remote times, before the arrival of the Inca Empire, every nation, village, corner, class and house had its own god. And among the numerous gods was the anaconda, reputed for its ferocity and cruelty". *Royal Commentaries of the Incas*, by Inca Garcilaso de la Vega.

Chacta

Many centuries ago, in Peru under the Inca reign, evil stamped its seal for eternity. It all began with a beautiful but sad story that took place in the Andes. The small city of Pacha Rurac, known to all as a land of plenty, stood as a prosperous, brilliant and peaceful society.

As the years went by, its rise unleashed the envy of the surrounding villages. Greed began to gnaw at the hearts of thousands of people and in the end the representatives of the various neighboring tribes decided to unite to destroy Pacha Rurac. Knowing beforehand that without outside help they would not be able to carry out their malicious plans, the representatives of these tribes agreed to turn to the most reputable shamans[3] of the region to ask for their support in the search

---

3   The shaman is presented as an intermediary or intercessor between man and the spirits of nature. He connects the world of the dead with that of the living and can be at the same time sage, counselor, healer and seer. He is often perceived as an initiate. He is the custodian of a specific culture of diverse beliefs and practices. He is mainly found in traditional ancestral societies, where he makes ornaments of his own while practicing in secret. His role includes a wide variety of functions, from tribal leadership, to ritual making, to healing illness, to plant knowledge, to direct psychic

for the forces of evil and thus form a solid and unbreakable alliance that would allow them to eradicate the city of Pacha Rurac and its inhabitants.

This is how they selected the best warriors and entrusted them with the delicate mission of bringing the spiritual masters with them. The veteran curacas[4], despite being aware of the terrible dangers facing the expedition, were blinded by their hatred for Pacha Rurac and decided not to warn them.

After several days of endless marching, the small group of soldiers finally reached the territory of the powerful shamans. Exhausted, they went to rest in one of the many caves hidden in the heart of the mountains. When they resumed their march, the paths were lost in stretches of land bordered by cliffs. Exhausted by the journey and suffocated by the dust of the earth, the brave explorers climbed the steep slopes of the mountain with great effort. Suddenly, a dull rumor forced them to look around.

Huge boulders falling from the mountain walls announced the approach of a terrible catastrophe. In a cold atmosphere charged with hostility, the stones were rolling towards the

---

action, to teaching or counseling. Generally, they have psychic powers and extrasensory perceptions such as telepathy, prescience, long-distance vision or divination.

[4] The curaca was an official of the Inca Empire who held the position of magistrate and had to ensure the prosperity of the empire. He was responsible for several family clans (*ayllus*) or groups of curacas. Among other things, he served as tax collector, but he was also responsible for the welfare of his taxpayers, whom he had to feed, house, clothe and equip. The curaca managed the agricultural surplus and all artisanal production. He also ensured that possible deficits were overcome and organized reserves for periods of scarcity - war, drought... -. In addition, it guaranteed the material security of orphans, widows and the sick and therefore possessed rights but also obligations. Holder of religious authority, he served as a mediator between the supernatural sphere and the realm of mortals. As such, he was held responsible in case of natural disaster.

expeditionaries, who were desperately fleeing in search of protection, but unfortunately the warrior who was leading them, blinded by a thick fog, took a false step and plunged vertiginously into a ravine, dragging with him his companions in misfortune towards a deadly fall.

The birds that witnessed the scene announced the tragedy to the shamans, leading them to the place of the drama, where they verified that everything was consummated. The daring expeditionaries were dead, the fear of their last moments could still be read in their twitching faces.

All these risks were not in vain, questioned the shamans, who immediately understood that these men were probably the bearers of an important message.

In the villages from which the expedition departed, twilight followed twilight and the expedition members still showed no signs of life.

"Maybe something bad happened to them," ventured a villager.

"Yes, the roads are steep and dangerous," said the tribal chief. Let's wait a little longer. Let's not jump to premature conclusions.

Thus began a long and agonizing wait. After several days the obvious prevailed: something serious had probably happened to the warriors. What to do? Send another expedition to certain death?

In the midst of the confusion, the curacas could not think of anything.

"It is necessary to deploy new soldiers, young and brave," said a priest of the group. There is no other solution. The presence of the shamans is necessary, otherwise the first expedition will have perished in vain.

"Stop fidgeting. After all, those shamans with immense powers will come by themselves," said a strange-looking individual, half sorcerer, half man.

Within weeks the omen was fulfilled. On a cold and foggy morning, the shamans arrived at the village wrapped in a cloud of dust. It was a group of strangers descending from the mountains, making the earth tremble with their footsteps. Upon recognizing them, the inhabitants crowded into the streets to receive such prestigious visitors with dignity.

Covered in brightly colored cloaks, the foreigners entered the village.

"We are the shamans of the mountains. We want to know why you have tried to contact us," said the one who seemed to be the leader of the group coldly.

"Some months ago we sent messengers, yes," the village chief replied humbly. But they never returned.

"Those men are dead. They desecrated the sacred mountains and paid for their audacity with their lives. Now, tell us what that important message was."

Silence prevailed as the curacas looked at each other, unable to utter a word. They were aware that their request was unusual. Not knowing how to approach such a momentous conversation, they took their time before answering and, to soften their prestigious visitors, the curacas placed baskets full of offerings at their feet.

They approached the delicate subject with caution:

"This is Pacha Rurac and..."

They were immediately interrupted:

"Ah, I see, I see..." commented the chief of the shamans. I read in your eyes your intentions....

Relieved by the answer, the curacas gave free rein to their hatred, thus exhibiting their purposes in the smallest details...

They spoke of sharing, of revenge, of a destruction followed by a better world, and the shamans, with black and perverse souls, listened with great interest to that speech saturated with hatred. And that was how the curacas who were plotting against Pacha Rurac made known their dire intentions.

After a long reflection, followed by a debate, it was the turn of the shamans to render their decision.

"We understand what you are trying to do and we are going to help you."

The pact was received with great enthusiasm by the villagers, and immediately a celebration was improvised for the prompt destruction of Pacha Rurac. Amidst all the merriment and joy, the most perfidious and cruel of all pacts was sealed. After the moment of pleasure came the more serious matters and the shamans, supported by the crowd, made sinister imprecations and sacrificed some beasts in order to invoke the forces of evil. But after all unimaginable efforts the attempt failed.

The forces of evil did not respond.

After arduous labor, they then proceeded to a special rite, but at its conclusion, the same famished results were revealed. In addition, a message was repeated incessantly: Chacta's presence was required.

He, the Benefactor of the Andes, had the necessary power to successfully complete the plan drawn up by the curacas. He was the noblest soul of the Andes, he had immense powers and possessed the ability to transform evil into good, manipulating it through time. She also alleviated the strangest illnesses that plagued those times. He revived small animals and healed the flock with his simple touch. With him, what was sterile became fertile. Chacta was the protected of the Sun God.

A legend circulated about him. It is said that, while still a child, he found a cave while playing hide and seek. He penetrated inside and there he discovered a dying bird. Chacta immediately took it in his hands and tried to revive it, but, in spite of his numerous attempts and good will, his efforts were in vain. The bird's cold, limp body told him that all was lost.

For the first time, Chacta was confronted with death. Unable to accept reality, he withdrew from the cave with tearful eyes, pleading with all his infant fervor to the Sun God to revive the little creature.

His request was so heartwarming that the Sun God himself approached him and made a solemn declaration:

"My child, your desire to do good is great, and your prayers are touching. To reward you, I grant you supernatural powers. Listen to me well, yes, very well: from today I grant you an energy that will allow you to control time in desperate cases. Thanks to this force, you will be able to go back to the past and alter the paths of destiny or the actions of men. If misfortune should fall somewhere, you will have the facility to stalk it and restore love and peace where it has disappeared. You will also be able to restore justice and health where they are absent. Finally, you will enjoy the authority to impose good where evil prevailed before."

The Sun God fell silent for a moment, and the Chacta boy felt divine energy flowing through his body, transforming him into a young man.

"From today, your duty will be to alleviate the suffering of living beings on earth. Keep in mind that if you misuse this gift, if you commit the slightest act of evil, your power will disappear immediately and you will be condemned to live out your existence in a sordid and gloomy world, amidst weeping, lamentations and regrets. You will bear the burden of your guilt for eternity until one day a noble and generous soul will free you from your burden. Have you understood correctly?"

The last words pronounced by the Sun god incited the young man to swear and commit himself, mad with joy.

"It is a great honor," he said to the sun god, thanking him for his complete trust and enormous generosity. Yes, I will live up to this privilege that has been bestowed upon me. I swear that until the end of my days my mission on earth will be to impart good.

After receiving such an extraordinary gift, Chacta devoted himself to his work. His mission began in the Andes, where he took it upon himself to visit the most remote villages, where the need for assistance cried out for his presence. His generosity was quickly recognized in every corner of the Andes.

Chacta not only cured the ailments of the body, but also those of the soul. A single glance was enough for him to penetrate the depths of the spirit, as well as the interior of the heart of each being. He understood what others could neither observe nor hear.

Frequently, his visits ended with this advice given in a tender voice full of wisdom:

"The invisible torments you, but it is your task to free yourself from this evil. Do not cling to that which harms your soul."

Chacta would place his hands on the patient and at simple contact the ailment that had afflicted him for years would disappear by enchantment. In other extreme cases, by the effect of a single breath, the dead recovered the life that had been taken from them. Wherever he went, the Benefactor of the Andes left relief and peace in his wake. Each cause further strengthened his motivation; doing good became his reason for living. Chacta had a mission on Earth and he vowed to respect and honor it until his last breath.

Thus he traversed the region incessantly, committing himself each day to foray into new trails, always ready to help and assist. Sometimes, when all seemed lost and he was tired of going round and round the narrow routes of the Andes, Chacta told himself that it would be much easier if he had someone to guide him, someone to show him the way. And as his thoughts were like an open book to the Sun God, the sky listened to his requests and a voice answered him.

> He who seeks from the dawn
> needs a good guide
> and, if you want to find your way,
> you should call Intillimay.

Chacta got the message. The so-called Intillimay was far from being unknown in the Andes; everyone knew that he was the most majestic and respectable condor in the territory. In the past, Intillimay had proved his fearlessness and bravery, and in the Andes he was feared and admired. Determined to listen to the voice that advised him, Chacta left his cave and set out in search of such a prestigious raptor.

For days he crossed mountains, valleys, ravines, streams and creeks and finally arrived at the lair of the king of the peaks and skies. The exaltation of his mission affirmed him, allowing him to tear away all his shyness. Thus it was that he went without further haste to the one who, according to him, was going to be his ally.

"I come to you, legendary Intillimay, to implore your help. My mission is entirely dedicated to helping others, but I need you as a guide, since, on many occasions, my steps have gone astray on the Andean trails or in the jungle and I have never reached my destination."

Intillimay found it hard to resist. The handsome young man in front of him showed so much determination and a look so full of candor and tenderness that it incited others to do good. The majestic condor accepted without hesitation.

From that day on, the two beings sealed an unbreakable pact, becoming inseparable friends. Over time, Intillimay learned to discover Chacta's world, dominated by purity and good deeds. Both imposed on each other workdays that began at dawn and ended at dusk.

They crossed the Andean territory through tortuous paths bordered by precipices. And a long line of patients awaited him every time Chacta returned to his cave, their gazes fixed on the sun, in silence, shivering from the tenacious cold of the region. Chacta would contemplate them and, full of compassion, would manifest himself.

"My happiness will never be complete as long as there are misfortunes on earth."

And he quickly devoted himself to his work.

It was only late at night when Chacta could finally glimpse a moment of rest. The protégé of the Sun God imposed himself to fulfill his duty by working relentlessly in order to fulfill his obligation, postponing his own care or rest until tomorrow.

One day, a group of men from I don't know where, shivering with cold, came to the threshold of the Chacta cave. They were dressed strangely, covered with a long alpaca cloak, wearing ostentatious attire, necklaces and bracelets in gold and silver. Upon seeing him arrive, they prostrated themselves at the feet of the Benefactor of the Andes and with an agitated voice, escaping from untuned throats, a cry burst from their lips:

"The world is lost!" they said in chorus. We come before you to implore your generosity. We beg you to cease your activities and accompany us. If you wish to avoid the destruction of the Andes, you must come with us.

Surrounded by these imaginative men, Chacta listened to them dumbfounded, surprised by their words and without understanding any of their confused intentions. To calm them down, Chacta invited them to enter his dwelling and prepared a coca tea to comfort them.

"Soon... very soon!" one of them repeated insistently. "Everything will be lost... Everything!"

These men were so mysterious... The expression on their faces, the evasive looks, the hand movements, the exaggerated gestures... Even their tongues were tongue-tied at intervals as they delivered the terrible message. Everything incited distrust.

Observing them in silence, Chacta remained silent, meditating for a long moment before coming to the conclusion that these terrible predictions were improbable. However, faithful to the precepts of generosity of heart, it was his duty to assist them.

In full reflection, a man broke away from the group mumbling some words and stood in the center shaking his head with circular movements, as if he wanted to impress him. In full agitation, the man was sweating profusely. He pulled a seashell out of one of his pockets and blew on it with all his might.

A mighty sound echoed, bursting forth in low, mournful resonances. It was like a cry of destiny, a warning that had reached its climax and was made available to those present. After a few seconds, the man with the snail stepped back imploring in a thousand ways.

"What an encounter!" Chacta concluded, "What if everything they say is true? They were men of flesh and blood describing probably a myth or a legend of times past. What they told could not be true. Listening to them, it was as if all the disasters of the world were about to befall the Andes.

Submerged in a deep sadness, Chacta mumbled to himself that this future would be meaningless, it would be like saying goodbye to this beautiful life and stopping his task in one breath; like preventing him from traveling the Andean routes with his faithful friend Intillimay to help the needy, to whom he unconditionally spread his love; like no longer having the support of the sun that had brought him so much pleasure and joy; like leaving this cave where he sheltered, the repository of many secrets and...

Stupefied, and with the purpose of ordering his ideas, Chacta walked more than a hundred steps in the narrow gallery. The message was confusing, and it was very difficult for the Benefactor of the Andes to accept these fateful predictions. "It is absurd," he kept repeating to himself. Finally, plunged in the greatest perplexity, he ended up declaring, "No, I can't go with you! I need time to reflect. I'm very sorry, but leave without me."

This was a transcendental event in his life, since, for the first time in his life, Chacta firmly refused to help his fellow man. Deep down, a mysterious force was forcing him to act in this way.

Despite the group's insistence, the Benefactor of the Andes did not give in. After having argued ad nauseam, having used all the unimaginable stratagems to convince him, his interlocutors left without obtaining his consent.

After his departure, Chacta imposed on himself a week of fasting and seclusion. He drank only valerian, praying from dawn to dusk to beseech his god to show him the way to the truth. Thus it was that, by dint of announcing destruction with so much anguish in their voices, the words of those men had deeply disturbed him. At the end of the forced retreat, Chacta left his refuge, determined to travel through the Andes to see with his own eyes if there were indeed reasons for alarm.

Dawn was rising under the auspices of a sunny day, and Chacta took different shortcuts to contemplate the various angles of the Andean territory. The mountains covered in their best attire undulated on the horizon, the song of the birds resounded in his ears and the soft air that circulated over the mountain tops confirmed that tranquility had long since prevailed in the region.

Chacta once again traveled the roads traveled by some Andean dwellers, and looked around the landscapes.

Indeed, he checked that there were no changes.

Calmer after that realization, Chacta returned to his cave. Nothing foreshadowed a possible disaster.

A few days later, some men showed up again, but this time covered from head to toe with a long cloak that went up to eye level, concealing their faces.

"It is to protect us from the cold Andean wind," said the strangers.

Chacta invited them to enter his cave and immediately lit a fire to warm them. In a short time, a sensation of heat filled the small cave due to the warm air coming from the fire. Despite the heat, the men did not shed their cloaks. It was impossible to see their faces. "Are they ashamed to show themselves?" wondered Chacta. Their gazes were elusive, as if they harbored the fear of being discovered. This attitude did not go unnoticed by the Benefactor of the Andes, but he barely had time to sit near the fire before the visitors manifested bringing a message of utmost importance. Then they lashed out with the same discourse as the group of alarmist men. With inordinate gestures of distress, they predicted chaos, serial disasters, until they concluded their speech in the same manner: Chacta was to accompany them.

"And what exactly were they talking about, what was the threat that weighed so heavily on the Andes? The picture was bleak and vague. Many unanswered questions.

It is said that impassivity leads to nothing and that every moment is ideal for action.

Shaken by the fanciful arguments, Chacta decided to accompany them to offer his assistance. But no sooner had they left the cave when a fine rain poured down on the Andes. Quickly passing from small showers to a deluge carrying stormy winds that darkened the sky. In the space of seconds, night fell over the Andes, making it impossible to move about.

"I'm sorry," concluded Chacta, running for shelter. "It is impossible for me to accompany you."

"You have just accepted," the men replied disappointedly. "You can't take it back."

"I am sorry," Chacta repeated again, "since I listen to the dictates of my heart I know when a decision is right or wrong, and this is not the right time to venture into the Andes. I will not go with you; it will be of no use to insist."

Chacta was upset that he could not explain himself better so as not to appear intransigent. Moments before, his lips had given his consent; however, his heart told him otherwise, forcing him not to respect his commitment. Embarrassed by this unjustified behavior, Chacta returned crestfallen to his cave without being able to clarify his position. Outside, the rain intensified and for several days the Andes suffered heavy precipitation under a gray sky.

And the visitors, far from lowering their rearguard, stood by the Benefactor of the Andes, continuing without discouragement with their unusual demands. They harrumphed again and again with the same speech, as if it were a fervent prayer during a procession. In the end, the strangers got what they wanted: to disturb the tranquility of Chacta, who, affected by so much commotion and so much insistence, decided to put an end to the farce. To carry out his purpose, the first thing he needed was to expel them in order to find some peace and quiet, but bound by the promise to do good, he gave in at the first attempt and, after several days of disorder and scandals, Chacta reconsidered his decision.

One fine morning he came out of his cave and lowered his eyelids to show his commitment. He was ready to leave.

Immediately, the men blindfolded Chacta, who was led away without knowing where he was going and uneasy about leaving without the company of his faithful friend Intillimay. Despite the demands, the Benefactor of the Andes accepted the restrictive conditions.

It took three days of walking to reach their destination. Chacta heard great sighs of relief confirming that her journey was over, while anonymous hands carefully removed the band over her eyes.

He surveyed the surroundings curiously.

He found himself in a vast, arid, wild terrain, with no plants or animals and a low temperature. This is how he discovered this new inhospitable, indifferent and uninhabited environment; however, something called his attention, because in this hostile environment lived a conglomerate of Andean peoples led by shamans who appeared before him representing the different nations. He welcomed and greeted with great reverence the one who would be his savior.

Beyond the reception procession was the shadow of the traditional temple, majestic and solemn.

Making his way amidst the harmless snakes that proliferated on the ground, Chacta advanced very cautiously before a satisfied crowd. A multitude of curious and faithful people crowded to receive the newcomer, who was showered with perfumes and incense mixed with the aroma of various ointments. All these scents filled the air.

"We are the messengers of the Andes," they explained, "We are gathered here to prevent misfortune from stalking our territory.

Chacta had heard those words before, but unfortunately he had not understood anything. He was immediately led to a shrine where the crowd was waiting. At every step he heard voices coming from the darkness mixed with prayers. He watched all those men covered in tattoos and mean looks demonstrating in another language. Without knowing it, Chacta was in the lair of the people bordering Pacha Rurac, gathered in an atmosphere of hatred and vengeance around a huge bonfire where they hurled imprecations and invocations towards the sky. By dint of deceit and gruesome stories, which went so far as to hold the inhabitants of Pacha Rurac responsible for all the evils on earth, the curacas convinced Chacta to be on their side.

In spite of the mysteries and contradictions that abounded in this world, the force of circumstances made the Benefactor of the Andes feel the duty to grant them an opportunity. With a solemn voice, the illustrious Chacta pledged to help them with all his being and heart.

His words received a tremendous welcome. The moment so long awaited by the crowd had finally arrived.

Without missing a beat, the shamans gathered around the altar and invited Chacta to join them. A bit disoriented, he kept his eyes on the shamans as he awaited their instructions. After a brief invocation, a woman appeared in the crowd and placed a ceramic vase, shaped like a death mask with gold eyes, on the altar.

Chacta and the shamans formed a circle around the altar and took turns placing their hands inside the vase. Inside was warm water mixed with a secret substance that the shamans had prepared to guarantee the success of the plan.

Soon after, small lumps formed on the surface of the vase as a faint vapor rose in the room. Satisfied, the shamans raised their hands.

That was the sign for the rite to begin.

The atmosphere was truly shocking. Immediately, Chacta realized that the beautiful plants hanging from the temple walls were actually a poisonous species that had been used to make the substance in the jar where everyone had moistened their hands.

With no more time to lose, the shamans sprinkled a few drops among the men in the crowd. As if possessed, these men closed their eyes and began to chant in a strange dialect; others smashed ceramic statuettes on the ground and walked barefoot over the fragments.

Chacta looked at them in surprise, mute before the strangeness of what he could not understand. "What is the use of this rite?" he wondered. Suddenly he was haunted by a strong conviction of being part of an ignoble cause. The sensation was unbearable to him.

The atmosphere was charged with shouts and lamentations. The shamans, who had been observing Chacta for a long time, guessed his intentions and stressed to him not to be discouraged, to continue and to respect the instructions they had dictated to him. But doubts tormented the Benefactor of the Andes and unanswered questions plagued him. Had he given in stupidly? What was he doing there surrounded by all that crowd?

In that moment of extreme tension, Chacta let his intuition lead him to reject the orders given by the shamans. This rite did not fit with his principles. He dried his hands roughly on his clothes and decided to leave, but the shamans redoubled their efforts and with trickery, cunning and honeyed words managed to reassure Chacta and convince him that the rite was for the good of humanity.

Not far from the temple stood the prayer stone where everyone used to gather or come to deposit offerings. This was the meeting place between the earthly spirits and heaven, where the sorrows were entrusted but also the greatest aspirations, hoping for relief from suffering. The shamans led Chacta to this sacred place and placed their hands on the cold rock. They all cried out for a better world.

And the result was as sudden as it was impressive.

The non-transferable powers of Chacta joined like a whirlwind with those of the shamans, and that energy reached a force of ten times greater, transporting itself with vigor from the earthly world to the beyond. But instead of doing good, as Chacta believed, the evil fluid directed by the malicious shamans awakened the forces of evil.

Ominous creaking sounds reached Chacta's ears, as if the trees had split in two. Suddenly, a furious wind rushed against the temple followed by a light rain that gushed towards the altar. A few minutes passed until the sky began to spit fire: this was the answer that the Pacha Rurac front people had been waiting for so long.

The flame of malice shone in the eyes of those demons. The link was established between the world of the living and the world beyond. The forces of evil, unleashed, prepared to go into action. Blinded by hatred and envy, the enemy peoples of Pacha Rurac prostrated themselves before the occult powers, kneeling on the ground to celebrate the new alliance and thank Chacta for his intervention.

Without knowing exactly what they were committing themselves to, they vowed to abide by the will of their new allies and humbly accept if in return they got what they wanted.

Chacta fell to the ground stunned and lost consciousness. He had given up everything to satisfy the shamans. When he finally regained consciousness, his feat was warmly praised and accompanied by an indescribable manifestation of rejoicing.

"What have I done to help them? I don't remember anything..." he added confused.

"Thousands of souls will be eternally grateful. You have fulfilled what we expected of you."

After having concluded the pact, the shamans, anxious to get rid of the Benefactor of the Andes, accompanied him to the door of the temple without further explanation and said goodbye to him full of joy. Chacta, still with a confused mind, was discarded as an object of little value and felt abandoned in a wasteland. His presence was no longer necessary.

Chacta advanced disheartened, looking around in amazement until he took a shortcut that led him back to his cave.

As he walked, he wondered what he had done to cause those beings to radiate so much joy on their faces. It was difficult for him to remember. He did not know if he had acted appropriately, for all he remembered was that he had participated in a rite, that he had become a pawn and, influenced by that strange atmosphere, had bowed to the demands of those shamans. In this state of total confusion he took the road back home in the hope of recovering in his habitat and resuming his daily life.

Pacha Rurac

Many centuries ago, a tragic story was the origin of the hidden secret of the Andes. Despite the envy and suspicion of the neighboring peoples, there was a flourishing kingdom composed of inhabitants full of goodness. It was Pacha Rurac, which shortly before its destruction was annexed by the Inca Empire.

Fascinated by the beauty of its landscapes and the warm welcome of its inhabitants, the Inca sovereign commissioned his best architects to build various public buildings and his most skilled agronomists to transmit the art of cultivation and the foundations of the terraces.[5]

In a short time the most beautiful structures were erected and abundant and varied harvests sprouted. Huge silos where grain was stored were observed everywhere, as well as solid dams that protected the city against the ravages of nature. Pacha Rurac's reputation in the agricultural domain, and especially ar-

---

[5] "The terraces are artificial agricultural terraces on the Andean slopes that serve to obtain useful land for planting. They made it possible to make better use of water, both rain and irrigation water, by circulating it through canals that communicated their different levels. With this measure they avoided at the same time the hydraulic erosion of the soil". Ref. Wikipedia. This page was last edited on 19 June 2019 at 18:04.

chitecturally, crossed valleys, mountains and forests to the heart of the smallest Andean villages.

The Inca sovereign, creator par excellence, as well as a good man, found it logical to share these riches with other conquered territories in order to strengthen the bonds of friendship and solidarity. The Inca himself entrusted this task to Aucari Rumi, the curaca of Pacha Rurac, who promptly organized expeditions to transport a good number of jute sacks full of food and woolen clothing to offer to less fortunate peoples.

Parallel to the acceptance of the Inca uses and customs that were imposed along Pacha Rurac, a temple was erected to worship the Sun God, the calendar with the religious festivities was established and a priest of the Inca Empire was appointed to reside permanently. Little by little a new belief was implanted, completely sweeping away the old ones, with the exception of only one. In spite of the submission of its inhabitants to the new sovereign, they energetically refused to part with their Chancay dolls.[6] The rumors that spread were that, according to the annals of the city, these dolls had long contributed to protect its inhabitants against all attacks, tragedies and sufferings in the past.

The Inca sovereign was displeased when he learned of the rebellious behavior of the inhabitants, he found this act of disobedience as an affront and a lack of recognition for all the good that he had sown in Pacha Rurac since his arrival.

He considered that an exemplary punishment should be inflicted; however, in order to pass a fair and balanced sentence,

---

[6]   "On the basis of a vegetable framework, the inhabitants of the Chancay civilization manufactured dolls and other objects covered with scraps of fabrics and various threads". Ref. Wikipedia. This page was last edited on 11 June 2019 at 02:11.

he asked his escort to present him with a Chancay doll to better examine the case.

The soldiers executed his order immediately and soon after presented him with one of these dolls. Upon taking it in his hands, a strange feeling of well-being invaded the sovereign and he immediately succumbed to its charm, thus losing the desire to sanction. Instead, he decided to accept the use of these dolls in Pacha Rurac. Since that act was considered outside the law, owning a doll did not hinder the inhabitants from continuing to worship the supreme Sun god and abide by the laws and taxes necessary for the progress and welfare of the inhabitants.

The origin of the protective dolls comes from the city of Chancay, a coastal town bordering the Pacific Ocean. In those sad days for the city of Chancay, the anguished people knew that the death of the young prince was near. The healer also knew it, but her gifts revealed the solution in the form of a strange vision: a doll? Although she did not quite understand what had happened, she made a doll according to precise instructions and materials. The result was a doll with supernatural powers.

After a long and meticulous work, the healer obeyed the dictates of her intuition and went to the palace to place the doll on the deathbed of the young prince. Her reputation was such that the sick man's parents left the healer alone with him and the mysterious doll. Hours later, the prince recovered and an explosion of joy spread through the city.

Back home, the healer realized that she was being followed and her intuition warned her that her life was in grave danger. She kept the secret of doll making in a quipu,[7] where each knot, each space, contained detailed instructions on how to make the

---

[7] 'Knot' in Quechua. Lacking the knowledge of writing, this instrument was used to administer. It is believed that the quipu served to transmit information.

dolls. Her caution was justified, for days later she was found dead in her home.

A priest discovered the quipu and set out to decipher it, but without mastering the complex science he could only make imperfect dolls with limited powers.

Later, after the great earthquake that devastated his city, the priest went to Ollantay's house located in Pacha Rurac, his best childhood friend. Ollantay and his companions, moved by the sad story of their visitor, escorted him back to the destroyed city and began the reconstruction of the collapsed houses. In the face of such generosity, and in gratitude to Ollantay and his companions, the priest made dolls as explained in the quipu of the healer. He conceived twenty-five thousand, with alfeñique legs and arms made of small pieces of cane wrapped with threads, dressed in jute, geometric faces with eyes full of curiosity and protective powers, which he then distributed among the inhabitants of Pacha Rurac.

In Pacha Rurac, the transformation of the Andean lands was similar to that of that city.

Two palaces were erected to house the Inca and his warriors.

The cobblestone streets, the ostentatious residences and the public buildings gave architectural renown to the agglomeration formerly called Chaupituta. When the work was completed, the Inca was dazzled by his creation and renamed it Pacha Rurac ('creator of the world').

Since then, the Inca decided to spend as much time as possible in Pacha Rurac which, far from losing its charm, he particularly appreciated its hot springs. His stays at Pacha Rurac were very frequent, to the point of — without forgetting his sovereign duties — installing his secondary residence there.

Later, force majeure would force him to organize an expedition to the interior of the empire in order to know the state of the annexed territories after his last conquests. The Inca departed with great pomp from Cusco, capital of the Inca Empire, for a few months in the company of the elite guard, not without putting at Pacha Rurac's disposal one of his selected regiments.

A few weeks after the Inca's departure, life in Pacha Rurac continued its normal course with no threat looming on the horizon.

But this serenity came to an end during a beautiful sunny day, when the townspeople encountered the intrusion of a gigantic cloud of black butterflies that hid the sky with their wings. Their size and number was such that darkness enveloped the city completely.

The winged creatures entered each house to the surprise of its inhabitants. Disquiet quickly took possession of their spirits. And their uneasiness was justified because, although the inhabitants of Pacha Rurac ignored it, those insects had been sent by the Çupaipa Huacin, who, blinded by envy and the prosperity of the city, reacted favorably to the multiple requests of the frontalero peoples. These unusual and vigorous insects, with large eyes, remained several days as if petrified on the walls of the houses without moving.

Although their color evoked death, after the surprise of the first hours, the inhabitants of Pacha Rurac, seeing them as harmless, accepted the new contingent in their territory. And life in Pacha Rurac resumed its course.

One day, however, that tranquility came to an end as parents and children were gathered at Aucari Rumi's house for a hearty lunch.

After finishing her meals, Cumac, Aucari's youngest daughter, thirteen years old, set off as usual with a troop of llamas towards the mountains. Arriving at the top, she sat down to contemplate

71

the surrounding nature and the city of Pacha Rurac at her feet. Everything was going as usual. Her dreamy mind was wandering peacefully when, suddenly, she was startled by a deafening noise that increased and tore her from her contemplative state.

The noise seemed to come from the city. Cumac tried in a thousand ways to catch with her eyes something that could help her identify the sound that had disturbed her so much, but unfortunately she could see nothing.

At that moment, a chilling vision shocked his body. Millions of black butterflies were fleeing from the dwellings of Pacha Rurac carrying with them the Chancay dolls, stripping their owners of their protections. Gripped by fear, Cumac was a nervous wreck. However, after a few moments, she decided to leave the mountain and run to her people. As she left, an immense bird of terrible appearance made an incursion into the Andean sky, casting its shadow over Pacha Rurac.

Almost plucked, its skin was a deep black. It possessed a crooked beak and six disproportionate legs with impressive claws. The hideous bird flew over Pacha Rurac uttering bloodcurdling wails that frightened its inhabitants. The scene was terribly disturbing, for danger lurked in the city.

Butterflies? A bird? That in another time and place might seem normal, but its hideous appearance was the manifestation of a plan painstakingly crafted in secret by the supreme leader of the forces of evil: the great anaconda. Hidden until it was time to return in triumph when the region was subdued.

"There is no more time to waste," Cumac muttered, trembling with fear.

Torn between living alone or perishing with her loved ones, Cumac chose to wander alone in this desolate universe and fled to hide from the sight of the bird and her troop of butterflies.

In Pacha Rurac, fear paralyzed the villagers. Aucari and his family were surprised to see that the butterflies that days before were petrified on the walls of each house now escaped from each dwelling with the most precious objects of the community. Tragedy was knocking at the doors and the Chancay dolls were their only protection.

In a cloud-laden sky, the butterflies stood in single file like an army that, at the command of their superior, obeyed the gigantic bird with the twisted beak without a murmur.

Disgruntled, the inhabitants watched with sadness the plundering of which they were victims. However, they were reassured to think that plundering twenty-five thousand dolls in one fell swoop was an impossible mission.

But the facts proved otherwise: the stubborn and industrious butterflies continued with their industrious duty and completed the assault with disconcerting speed. Suddenly, these malicious insects had become a threat they could not ignore.

Forming a line, the butterflies followed the dictates of the black bird. That bird with its twisted beak described wide circles in the sky of Pacha Rurac as if it were trying to delimit a territory.

"What can we do?" asked the dejected villagers.

They were not warriors who could defend their village against an assault, nor did they possess weapons that could prevent the untimely attack of the butterflies. They were mere mortals devoid of malice.

The moment was crucial; his helplessness, total.

And, when all seemed lost, the regiment that the Inca had assigned to defend Pacha Rurac made its appearance. Overflowing with security and confidence, hope was reborn in the hearts of the inhabitants. Armed with bows and arrows, including spears, they quickly took the main square following the commander's instructions. From there they launched the first flight of arrows, although without success; the targets were flying at high altitude and the archers understood that it would be difficult to reach them.

Faced with the failure of those experienced warriors, Aucari was certain that he would never see the Chancay dolls again; in spite of this, he tried to appease his fellow citizens with comforting words.

"We've had a bad encounter, but it's in the past. That bird won't bother us anymore. Don't worry, the butterflies will return with our dolls," Aucari concluded.

"Too beautiful to be true," replied Ollantay. "But I wonder, why didn't we react before?"

Ollantay was one of the most faithful servants of the curaca Aucari of Pacha Rurac. With a rebellious temperament, he did not hesitate to expose his point of view, even if it contradicted his boss. If he judged it necessary, he acted according to his own intuition, even if he had to withdraw from authority. In the face of adversity, his temperament never gave way; on the contrary, he took it as a new incentive to resume the fight.

The young Ollantay did not hesitate to get involved in defending just causes, and it mattered little if the situations were adverse to him. Effusive, extroverted, he shared the joys as well as the sufferings of his people.

"Why didn't we react sooner?". Multiple questions, and Aucari couldn't manage to answer them. With great sadness, the families had to resign themselves to watching their dolls disappear into the sky. The big bird headed north and vanished followed by its sinister retinue of black butterflies.

Hardly had the crowd begun to disperse when the earth shook. The quake shook the city with such force that panic spread among the townspeople still grieving over the theft of their protections.

Faced with the new test they were facing, Aucari tried to calm them down:

"Don't panic! Gather your families, this tremor won't last long! Cheer up!"

While the houses were swaying dangerously, entire families converged towards the central square. The most solid constructions crumbled with thunder, screams of terror and pain mingled, calls for help exploded from every corner.

And the worst was yet to come.

After a few minutes of trembling, the dam fragmented. The men standing nearby had no time to warn the rest of the inhabitants, soon after the dam gave way to the violent shaking of the earth's crust and the water, an essential element for life, flowed freely through the streets of the town. Cold, frothy and terrifying. It swept over Pacha Rurac like a monstrous wave.

From the top of the mountain, Cumac watched the earth tremble beneath his aching feet. The large silos were the first victims of the destruction, and grains, stones, branches, mud and objects of all kinds formed a thick substance that spread through the city.

A loud noise of stones rolling down the mountain made Cumac shudder. Panic-stricken, the little Rumi girl could only watch the tragic events that marked the end of Pacha Rurac. Never in her life had she been confronted with so much pain. Helpless, she chose to pray with all her strength and devotion to the Sun God, begging him to deliver her community from this cruel disaster. But the fervent fervor was not enough and the destruction continued. The spectacle was even more terrifying for Cumac because to what his eyes witnessed was added what his ears heard: the heart-rending screams, the cries of all those poor families... Their parents, their playmates, their neighbors..., all without exception were desperately struggling to preserve their lives, praying and imploring. With faces drenched in tears.

And to make matters worse, the coup de grace had not yet sounded. A huge noise made her turn around and, when she looked up, Cumac saw a huge block of ice falling from the mountain, unstoppable towards Pacha Rurac...

"How to warn them... Oh, God Sun, why should so many innocent people suffer?"

Finding no consolation for his bitter tears, Cumac cried out to heaven. Meanwhile, the terrified villagers of Pacha Rurac watched as the ice avalanche headed toward them like an implacable armada. Fear intensified and the inhabitants, knee-deep in water, ran in panic with no precise trajectory. Parents desperately searched for their children, children begged for them in tears. Families scattered and gathered together in desperation trying to console each other. It was chaos.

Aucari did everything in his power to reassure them, and after several unsuccessful attempts, he asked the inhabitants to gather in the square to pray fervently in the hope of being heard by the Sun God.

Death continued its work. The killer tidal wave composed of ice, stones and mud spread over the city, hitting it with fury and invading the streets, public establishments, parks and residences. In the blink of an eye, its inhabitants were buried. A dense, gray layer covered them.

Little by little, a terrifying silence settled in. The silence of death.

The only survivor was Cumac, who could not understand how everything had disappeared in such a short time.

"It's a nightmare! A terrible nightmare! Nothing but a nightmare!"

The moment the earth stopped shaking, Cumac descended from the mountain with his animals.

Despite the total destruction of Pacha Rurac, evil had not given its last word. To complete his work, a multitude of luminous objects emerged from the sky and fell like a rain that fulminated the earth. Cumac watched them fall in a precise order, accompanied by light flashes. On contact with the earth, they sank into it.

Still in shock, Cumac did something irrational: she ran like lightning and caught one of these luminous objects in her hands before it became part of the bowels of the earth. To her surprise, it was a magnificent funerary mask finely worked in gold, inlaid with precious stones in the shape of a charm. What she did not know was that all these sunken masks demarcated a territory.

Like an automaton, Cumac picked up the mask and hid it in one of the pockets of her skirt, although without knowing why she was doing so. Meanwhile, restless and abandoned, she told herself that she was at the mercy of a bloody fate, marked by pain and despair. Her painful tears plunged her into deep sadness, for in Pacha Rurac she was leaving her soul. Trembling and inconsolable, she left the city to inform the Inca and ask for his help. Crossing mountains, dodging precipices and crossing valleys, riverbanks, mountains and suspension bridges, Cumac let herself be guided by her flame to Cusco, capital of the Inca Empire.

After several days of walking on the tortuous paths of the Andean routes, he found by chance the route used by the Inca's retinue. After being informed, the monarch went in person to Pacha Rurac.

Upon arrival, he and his soldiers were incredulous at the extent of the disaster. Nothing was left standing. Shattered buildings, animals and families decimated, missing and, above all, that suffocating silence where once stood a prosperous, peaceful and full of life city. Only a little girl deprived of tears had survived. Convulsed, the Inca could not hold back his tears. Nothing remained of his work. However, he was proud of it. In those terrible moments, the Inca decreed Pacha Rurac a sacred place and ordered to build a huaca at the entrance of the city, an immense mortuary monument in the form of a circular tower to bury the dead. The tower was the most beautiful of all and so large that it rivaled a small fortress.

After several weeks of intense labor, the soldiers finished with the painful task of extracting bodies from the rubble to place them in the huaca, thus respecting the designs of the sovereign Inca. The main function of the structure was to protect the souls of the deceased from evil. All the actions were focused on assuring the inhabitants of Pacha Rurac an eternal rest in the Hanan Pacha. [8]

After covering the earth with his tears, Cumac disappeared forever. The searches carried out at the request of the Inca to find her whereabouts were in vain. To forget her painful condition of orphan, Cumac took refuge in the most inhospitable place of the Andes and there she established her home, near Pacha Rurac.

[8] 'Sky' in Quechua.

The Apparition

At Helébora's house in Cuchimilcos, the days go by and the anguish of not knowing where to start is gaining weight. She feels helpless in an unknown place. However, what is about to happen is going to surprise her, as strange events will cloud the quiet life of the two women.

On repeated occasions, Helébora has the impression that she is not alone; light breezes of air circulate through the house, going round and round, creating small whirlwinds, seriously disturbing her. At times, she thinks she is close to dementia. Sometimes, sitting at the table while sipping a hot herb, she remarks that the rates move slightly. Her mother, who has also remarked on the disturbances in her home, tries to play them down so as not to reveal her visible bewilderment.

*****

From the bowels of the earth, the spirits awaken one by one from their long and forced sleep. Accustomed to the darkness, the spirits make their way in disorder, moving with difficulty, towards the enchanting voice that has brought them back to the world. One by one, they open their seductive eyes and discover their new environment. Breathing the mountain air, they recognize the land where they were born.

"How many changes!"

"Hello! Is anyone here?"

Their voices are so faint that the echo collides involuntarily and gets lost in the air. The tanned complexion of Aucari the curaca of the group, shows a well-tempered character, his presence alone instilling respect and admiration. Well-groomed in appearance, he wears a wool tunic with feline motifs, a sumptuous cloak embroidered in gold and silver, and on his head rests a crown adorned with multicolored feathers from rare species. Aucari is the first to enter Helébora's home. Shortly after, the women are introduced.

Dressed in long, simple and austere tunics with some embroidered with golden edges, they wear their hair tied with colored wool ribbons. Most of them wear necklaces of precious stones. The men, children and elders are all dressed in the same way: simple long tunics, without any surcharge, and small borders sewn with silver thread.

"Is this where I'm going to live?" Aucari asks himself in a bit of a daze.

Covered with the dust accumulated over the centuries, the spirits look inside the house when they hear the door creak and feel the contact with the cold air of the Andes. One by one, they enter the house, shaking off the dust they have been carrying for an eternity.

*****

Helébora, withdrawn in her thoughts, does not notice the transformations that are slowly taking place in her house. The dirtiness of the place bothers her. Her mother, approaching her daughter, argues that it is nothing that cannot be solved. Broom in hand, she sweeps the furniture, floors, corners, ceilings and walls, picking up most of the dust.

But the next day the amount of dust has doubled. Fortunata shakes her head in amazement, noting with surprise the never-ending task that awaits her. No sooner has she finished the first round than the mounds of dust pile up again. Cleaning must be done every half hour.

It is unthinkable to put an end to the chores. Striving to keep calm, Fortunata shakes and shakes, to the point that, with a choked and complaining voice, and eyes irritated by so much dust, she begins to develop a strange aversion for her own home that forces her to leave it. Alone. Helébora, shaken by barely audible diaphanous voices, chooses to stay at home.

The strange mounds of dust are completely installed in the house. Helébora is filled with horror at being threatened by this amount of dust that piles up even in the most discreet corners, so dense that she has difficulty moving her legs. Uncomfortable with the foul air in her house, Helébora also leaves her home before asphyxiation deteriorates her condition.

"What a horrible feeling! Impossible, I can't stay at home."

*****

Spirits prowl the surroundings with a look of times past, discovering with wonder the outside world.

"How life has changed."

"The world is not the same," says another.

"I feel like a foreigner in my own land."

"Yes, but the pure air fortifies us."

"Blow on me. Please blow on me," says another, showing his right ear. I want to hear the sound of earthly life and be sure I won't turn to ashes or blow away in the wind.

With eyes dilated by so much novelty, the spirits emerge from the bowels of the earth with their arms raised high. Enraptured, ecstatic, believing themselves to be the owners of this world, they explore inch by inch those lands where they were born. Extremely excited, with a contagious joy, they share special moments for the community.

"The world has been transformed," some repeat with unbridled surprise.

"No, the world is the same. It is we who have changed. Do not forget that we are spirits now."

"Look, some sections of the Inca routes are still preserved."

"But the suspension bridges are gone."

"These men live like barbarians! With no respect for the legacy of the past... Fortunately, the flames survive."

"Let us rejoice that after having been submerged for centuries we have returned to the surface and the light of the sun will guide our actions. Enough philosophizing, let's not waste any more time and let's get down to work."

*****

Disoriented, Helébora remains inert on the outskirts of her home, when shortly afterwards, shaken, she feels a gust of wind penetrate her house and, in the blink of an eye, the dust blows the old gate and the windows wide open. In the last few minutes, a light warm breeze blows through the surroundings and a pleasant feeling comes over her. Now, the gentle wind invites her to return home. With her ears tuned and her eyes wide open, Helébora walks through the rooms of her home to see that nothing has changed. Only, she thinks she feels that an Andean mystery is manifesting itself in her.

*****

The compact spirits have managed to infiltrate the girl's home, pushing each other roughly trying to find the best possible space. Ollantay and his son move closer to Helébora to welcome her. On that special day for the Pacha Rurac community, Ollantay spreads out like a seagull in flight and is repeatedly tempted to take the initiative and move an object to be warned. Unfortunately, the priest Aucari prevents him from doing so, arguing that it would be an abominable mistake to make himself known.

*****

As soon as Helébora brushes against Aucari, he lowers his arm in a sign of approval. The priest looks at the girl with intensity and feels that the fateful moment has arrived. Then he looks back at his community, lowers his head and raises his arms. This is the sign everyone was waiting for: the spirits gently strike their chests with their hands, bringing to light a very fine, almost invisible golden dust that remained stuck to their bodies. The dust carries the most precious memories: the dolls. This dust now swirls delicately around Helébora. Unexpectedly, the faces of the Chancay dolls permeate the young girl's memory at an astonishing speed. They parade in their best attire, showing the smallest detail of their tailoring.

"These dolls are very ugly; they look very unpleasant!" Helébora says to herself, "Who's going to want them?"

"That's precisely what it's all about," Aucari explains. Despite their lurid appearances, Chancay dolls have served in ancient times as amulets, endowed with magical powers to fiercely protect their lord and master. Remember, girl, appearance is only artificial, what matters is what lies deep within each being.

*****

Helébora feels a sense of urgency. Suddenly, she hurries to find the little earthenware jar where her mother preserves her savings for the year. Without informing her mother, and taking advantage of the fact that she is with Don Gumersindo, she goes to the market. Arriving at the little shop of embroidery and fabrics, Helébora hurriedly picks up some pieces, a pair of scissors, colored threads, needles, markers, skeins of wool. Forming a small pile with the utensils, she presents them to the saleswoman.

"I'll take it all. Please wrap it in paper."

The saleswoman, knowing the needs of Helébora and her mother, was surprised that this young girl had obtained such money. In her few conversations with her mother, the saleswoman was sure that these two women were living a life of deprivation. Suddenly, the daughter comes to her with this bundle of money and, without haggling, cancels the merchandise in full. Ambivalent, the saleswoman is inclined to refuse the transaction, while, inside her, the need presses her. Closing her eyes, she finally gives in and accepts the order.

Back home, he finds his mother preparing lunch.

"Where have you been, Helébora? I've been looking for you for over an hour. And this? What are you doing with all those fabrics?"

"Mom, I bought them with the money you kept in the clay jar."

Upon hearing her daughter's confession, Fortunata receives one of the hardest blows of her life. That money is the fruit of countless hardships and its use was intended only to preserve the identity viscerally linked to the land where they were born. And Helébora knows this very well. Fortunata does not understand that her daughter has consummated such an act without any remorse.

"Helébora, you knew very well the usefulness of that money. I instilled it in you since you were a child. But now you have just killed all my hope, and yours too."

"If I dared to take it, it is precisely to ensure my presence at the fair."

"You've lost your mind! Come on, return all this material now."

"I won't do it, mom. I'm going to show up at the fair and believe me: I'm going to pay you back all the money, down to the last penny. I have the impression that a supernatural force has pushed me to make this decision."

"Please, daughter. Stop using supernatural forces as a pretext."

"Mom, it's not a game. Remember that you have always told me that our past is important. That money will allow me to make our roots known, not only to our family, but to visitors to the fair. He will come alive with the dolls I will create."

"Making our roots known" is like a peal of bells announcing change. A sign of joy and tranquility nestles in Fortunata. She never imagined this would happen, but Helébora has touched the most sensitive strings of her heart. Standing in front of her daughter, she looks at her with eyes full of tenderness and, abandoned in her thoughts, Fortunata remembers as if it were yesterday her great-grandmother, her grandmother and her mother passing on the ancestral tradition. Telling stories, respecting the cults, preserving the festivities of their ancestors, instilling their customs and traditions to future generations. Now, Helébora is ready to take over. The wonderful thing is that, with her extraordinary imagination, she will transmit the tradition like no one else, bringing to a larger audience those stories and legends of a whole generation.

Fortunata cannot stop him.

"I'm an idiot. Normally any mother would be proud to hear her daughter with such determination and perseverance to defend what belongs to her: her past. And look how I react. Go ahead with your idea, Helébora. From now on you will have my full support."

The dull worries fade away, and Fortunata laughs with conviction as she hugs her daughter with all her might. Helébora, for her part, shares her worries and fears. No one can predict what will happen, but one thing is certain: she will fight until the last moment to preserve what is hers.

The next day, the burning desire to start the confection haunts her, to the point of distracting her from her daily chores. Helébora no longer counts the llamas or makes sure they have all eaten enough to descend from the mountains on their way home. Images of the dolls accompany her on the silent stretch. Fleeting faces appear before her, offering her a myriad of details. At times, Helébora has the impression of seeing them sitting on the huge stones that rest on the stretch that leads her home. Her visions push her to run to catch them, and only the displeasure of an abrupt collision forces her to come to her senses.

*****

In the last few minutes, light gusts of wind give way to countless spirits that, flying around the little house of yellow flowers, gather disorderly at the lintel of the gate. Annoyed and full of anger, Aucari stops at the threshold and, with his golden rod in hand, harshly reproaches the indiscipline of his people. He beat them from left to right, and then he went in search of the perpetrator of this act until he managed to corner him. The latter, seeing himself besieged by his leader, communicates the interest that has induced him to commit such insubordination.

Ollantay, strangled by a strong melancholy, incites all those present to return to the interior of the house. After having listened to the sentenced man, Aucari gives him a severe correction and addresses the group ordering the progressive entrance. After a few moments, the twenty-five thousand souls gather in the room.

Whispers and conversations from different sides multiply, and Helébora, who has just arrived, is certain to hear strange noises. Immediately, Aucari instructs the loom experts to position themselves at Helébora's level. Equipped with needles, threads and period instruments, the textile masters guide the young woman in the execution of her work.

*****

Suddenly, invisible hands direct the making. The design, the pattern cutting, the fabrics, the colors to be used, the basting... Helébora is surprised to see that the work is done by itself.

It is just beginning to get dark and the girl continues her work in awe. The finishes are prepared with exquisite care: eyes, hair and mouths are expressive as she listens to diaphanous voices imparting directives and advice. The textile masters check the finished dolls. Between stitching and spinning, Helébora concludes, doll by doll, her successful work.

*****

It is barely six o'clock in the evening when in Pacha Rurac, in the Kingdom of Darkness, the anaconda rises from its long slumber. Only a significant event can bring about a change in his behavior. For several minutes, a tenacious pain has been afflicting him, the multiples needles that enter and leave her wrists disturb her organism. The spirits, sewing with enough yarn, stitch with the purpose of obtaining a perfect finish.

Between jabs and jabs, the anaconda is certain that his life hangs by a thread. In a sea of bewilderment and between twists and turns to alleviate his complaints, the beast orders his guards not to let any foreigner enter.

"The past haunts me!" she cries out in anger. "It has come to my kingdom and I cannot allow it."

Desperately leaving her palace, the anaconda has enveloped herself in an air of anger and contempt for the human race. After vacating her throne of skulls and skeletons, she wanders through the labyrinths of her kingdom with a thirst for vengeance, her merciless tail lashing out at the unfortunate people in the vicinity.

"It's as if my defeated enemies are returning from the realm of the dead!" exclaims the beast in a daze. "I must stop it!"

The pain comes to him as he continues his walk through the shadowy, pestilent recesses of his kingdom.

"No! I am not willing to share my reign."

For the first time in centuries, a feeling of fear tortures her and the nervous movements of her tail shake the land of Cuchimilcos.

*****

Helébora is separating the cloths when, with the first shaking of the earth, she leaves her house in anguish to find that the whole town has taken to the streets.

"The earth is shaking! Can you feel it, Mom?"

"Yes, and I hope it stops soon. If it doesn't, I don't know what will become of me, daughter."

Haunted by the tragic events that tarnished her childhood, that woman with nerves of steel begins to weaken. Fortunata embraces Helébora tightly as if she were saying her last goodbye.

*****

Aucari does not want to say it for fear of needlessly alarming the group, but, lost in his thoughts, he advances towards the outside of the enclosure where he is informed of what has happened. The tearful and fearful faces of the inhabitants speak for themselves. After a brief fright, the earth stops shaking and the inhabitants, now calmer, return to their homes. A pestilential stench spreads through the air, the same foul odor of that sad day when he and his community were englued, Aucari corroborates his doubts and, before such evidence, communicates his suspicions to his people.

"We were reckless. We forgot that, after six o'clock in the evening, we had to cease all activity on earth. The anaconda has awakened from its long slumber: the Kingdom of Darkness is on alert. Come on, let's hide all the fabrics, threads and dolls in those Inca vases. Let's get to work, we must get away from Cuchimilcos."

*****

As soon as she opens the door to her room, Helébora is struck by the unusual spectacle: scissors, threads, needles, fabrics, patterns, finished and unfinished dolls are suspended in the air. They move in a line. The cortege makes its way to the living room and delicately descends to hide in the pair of Inca vases that her mother keeps in the living room. Thinking she is living a dream, Helébora rubs her eyes again and again in the hope that it is only an illusion. But faced with the harsh reality, she is certain that she is surrounded by Andean spirits.

"I'm going crazy."

Frightened, she warns her mother of what is happening. Fortunata, who has never seen her daughter in such a state, accompanies her to the room to witness that everything is just as they had left it, and that the fabrics and accessories recently purchased by Helébora are in the Inca vessels.

"Helébora, knowing you as you are, surely you have ordered the material and then put it in the glasses. I think the trembling of the earth has upset you a little, daughter. You'd better rest."

That night Fortunata sleeps next to her little girl. Helébora wants to explain her fears, but nothing coherent comes out of her mouth. Not daring to sleep, the daughter stays awake imagining that spirits will come to harm her. Everything indicates that mysterious forces dwell beside her.

*****

Under Aucari's orders, the operation to hide the wrists lasts a few minutes.

"Now we can return to our usual shelter," says Aucari. Quickly! Before the anaconda notices and finds us.

Back at the Inca huaca, Aucari is satisfied to know everything hidden and thanks the community for their work when, in the background, remarking something unlikely, a member of the community tenderly wrings out a piece of cloth. As he approaches, Aucari recognizes where it came from.

"What are you doing with that piece of cloth?"

"It fills me with nostalgia," Ollantay replies with a nostalgic air. "When I lived in Pacha Rurac, my doll was made with the same fabric."

Aucari listens to him coldly. Once again this character with disheveled hair risks Helébora's job. Furious and exalted, he curses the hour when this troublesome spirit returned.

"You are reckless! With this error of judgment, you are compromising Helébora's submission to the contest. If we return, we will be discovered by the anaconda, damn it! Take courage because at this very moment you are coming with me; we must place that piece of cloth with the others."

*****

The anaconda, in discomfort for a few moments, continues its search. He must find the culprit and will not rest until he finds him. However, when he gets no answer, he sets out on a journey to the top of the mountains. He needs to know the truth of the facts and for this he goes to the Oracle, to ask for the help of the feline eyes that he has used so much to discard any spirit that opposes his purposes.

After centuries of lying in the dark, its massive tail has grown to unimaginable proportions, lashing the roads, breaking them and uprooting trees along the way. At the top of the mountain, he requests an audience with the Oracle. The latter is surprised to see this animal in his realm and asks him dryly:

"What brings you here, anaconda?"

"About half an hour ago I felt very strange pangs in my body, as if thousands of needles were pricking me, hurting my skin, penetrating my blood vessels, drawing my blood..."

"The remorse is great, and the guilty conscience doesn't leave you alone, anaconda."

"I come to implore your help, Oracle."

"How can I be of service?"

"Lend me the feline eyes, I'll give them back to you as soon as I finish my expedition on earth. I promise."

"Expedition? You know you're not allowed to wander the earth."

"I ask your indulgence. Danger stalks my kingdom, for I am certain that the spirits of ancient times have returned."

"Spirits? You're delirious, anaconda."

The Oracle sets his eyes on the vastness of the sky and imagines the myriad of changes on earth that such a situation would bring about.

"I shouldn't have to. From the day you colonized this territory, haughty anaconda, you promised to fend for yourself. However, as an act of kindness, I will grant you what you ask. But remember, you will only get this first and last favor from me."

"It's all right. You have my word."

A brightness descends from the sky that blinds the anaconda for a few moments. In its face it feels the feline eyes, ready to be used. This is how the beast undertakes its first incursion into Andean territory after centuries of convalescence. His field of vision has increased and he is able to observe kilometers and kilometers of terrain. The culprit of its discomfort has no chance to hide. The anaconda advances meticulously, dismantling houses, farms, vacant lots, mountains and any other obstacle it encounters.

*****

Shortly before the anaconda begins its search with feline eyes, Aucari and Ollantay find themselves on dry land. Between mountains and stones, there is a long stretch separating the huaca and the village of Cuchimilcos, and Aucari unceremoniously scolds Ollantay for his behavior.

Suddenly, Aucari stops in the middle of the road, troubled by the strange phenomenon his eyes witness. The narrow worn paths seem to fog up little by little with a stale air. Between the abysses and natural hazards, a black smoke like a dirty shadow covers the tortured environment. Looking up at such a sad spectacle, Aucari glimpses the anaconda, wagging its tail back and forth in an outburst of destruction wherever it passes. The images of evil are lost in the confusion and terror of that instant and the animal's pestilent exhalations submerge the Andes in a sea of filth.

For an instant, Aucari thinks about getting emboldened and reprimanding the anaconda that it is not allowed to tread the earth. But then she comes to her senses. Unfortunately, Aucari must not arouse suspicion and reluctantly agrees to stay hidden.

The storm unleashed by the beast prevents the two spirits from advancing quickly. The foul, thick air unleashed by the beast obstructs the passage of the spirits and the wind, laden with scrap metal, pebbles and objects of little value, throws everywhere its overwhelming gifts while the spirits continue their arduous ascent up the steep and abrupt territory where the little house of yellow flowers stands.

"And to think that destiny had set this new civilization on golden crockery for us. Now it is finished. Thanks to your legendary recklessness and this piece of cloth, the anaconda will soon discover everything, and our presence on earth will be of no interest," laments Aucari, choked with grief.

"We don't have to give up so quickly, sir. Let's continue."

"Impossible! The beast wears the feline eyes of the Oracle. It is sure to find us."

Aucari cannot bear this sad end. Distressed by the difficulty of advancing, and imagining the kind of punishment he and his people will suffer when they are discovered, he continues to advance in the company of Ollantay. With a cry of despondency, they both plunge to meet their terrible fate amidst the mournful whistling of the wind, the merciless voice of the anaconda, flying objects, tree branches and uprooted trunks. In desperation, Aucari runs into the animal's tail and is forced to jump up and down to avoid being hit.

"It's useless! We have to run away from here. It is useless for us to stay if our destiny is written."

In a few seconds, the animal's tail whips Aucari's back and the pain is so intense that the curaca falls unconscious to the ground. Ollantay comes to his rescue and, covering himself with a sheet of paper that floats in the air, manages to drag his master away. Half stunned, Aucari manages to open his eyes.

"Oh, I can't stand this pain!"

"Sir, can you stand up? Come, lean on my shoulder."

"What a mess! In a matter of minutes, it will all be over."

"But, sir, this is the moment to show our courage. Let us continue."

"No! I can't do that. My duty above all is to make sure that the anaconda does not harm our community. I must take refuge in the huaca and warn of this sad reality."

Their character is broken when they see that they will be discovered. The facts are more than revealing: they have no escape.

With each step, the obstacles increase and the anaconda advances. Compressed with pain, Aucari tries to get up, groping through the thick air, and allows himself to be dragged along. Inside the whirlpool, the curaca reflects on what he could have achieved if none of this had happened. Ollantay offers him a tree branch, begging his lord to hold on to it. The whirlpool loses intensity and that is when the feline eyes warn the anaconda of the presence of intruders.

"If we don't get out of here we will be condemned to burn in the flames for all eternity," Aucari shouts in despair.

These flames emerge from all sides, tenaciously advancing toward them. The blurred images of the beast's disfigured body draw closer. An unknown inner force propels Ollantay to move at a faster pace. He uses a branch to perform his feat, reaching into the tumultuous whirlwind to grasp his master with a strong and vigorous hand. At that moment, barely conscious, Aucari feels the sky fall away and the world ceases to exist.

"May it be what the sun god wills," Aucari moans.

After an unprecedented struggle to free themselves, a gust of wind blows them out of the whirlwind and Ollantay manages to escape unscathed, with his curaca on his shoulders, to the nearest mountainside. Soon after, the two spirits are safe and sound, far from the anaconda's field of vision.

"Do you realize, Ollantay? We can't stay here any longer, we must leave."

"No, sir! We cannot leave, we are very close to reaching our end."

"You are always so stubborn. If you wish, you can stay, but I abandon this combat. We will never be able to deposit this piece of cloth in the Inca jar. Let the inevitable happen."

"Sir, please continue."

"Impossible, Ollantay. You yourself have witnessed the setbacks we have gone through. We cannot even move freely, for this foul air prevents us from doing so. It is useless. We will not arrive and it is better to give up now that we have not yet been discovered."

It is inevitable. Aucari desists in his task of hiding the last piece of cloth inside the Inca vase. Ollantay continues.

For one last time, both spirits listen to the movements of the beast. The brief tranquility ends, and Aucari departs with a deep emptiness in his being, an indescribable helplessness. Upon returning to the huaca, the entire community awaits them impatiently, and Aucari approaches his people with a sorrowful semblance to tell them what has happened.

"Things did not happen as we thought. We have lost, now all that remains is to return to our immobile and frigid state of yesteryear. Unfortunately, reality has hit us quickly without the necessary time to prepare ourselves."

In the huaca, moments of anxiety are experienced while the spirits watch their curaca with emotion. Dumbfounded by the sad news, they accommodate each other, preparing for eternal sleep. A sleep they should never have broken.

Ollantay

That same night, on the steep and uneven roads of the sierra a few kilometers from Cuchimilcos, the anaconda waves its sinister silhouette as it moves through the wasteland. Still without a clue. Stunned in thought, the beast is agitated by the fear that the ancient inhabitants of Pacha Rurac have inflicted these terrible sufferings on it.

*****

With the resignation of Aucari, Ollantay finds himself alone in a world full of transformations where he is the one who must face this explosion of changes. Terrified that his people would fall back into a vegetative state, he bravely faced the storm of winds that swept through the territory. Abandoned in this labyrinth, Ollantay no longer believes in miracles.

*****

In the little house with yellow flowers, Helébora is in a daze. Deep down, it would have been healthy for her to scream at the top of her lungs about what she has just seen. Finally, she plucks up her courage and walks out of the bedroom with a lamp in her hand towards the front door. What he observes makes his hair stand on end and gives him goose bumps, terrible threatening winds sweep at breakneck speed through the ramshackle and decayed roads of his village. Fear has enveloped the inhabitants in an irrational fear.

Leaving your home is very risky; asking for help is impossible. Cuchimilcos is full of precipices. Resigned to doom and obeying her mother's insistent calls, Helébora closes the door again and returns to her room in search of relative safety.

*****

Experiencing a feeling of regret, the anaconda continues its search for the source of its discomfort. It advances along truculent and tightly packed paths, thrashing its tail all over the place. Progressing with the arrhythmia of its pulsations, its giddy footsteps get lost in the hills. Suddenly, incongruous visions are projected in his brain. The feline eyes highlight the path leading to Cuchimilcos. The anaconda lacks a concise idea, but at the warning it unfolds its vigorous body in the direction of that remote village far from civilization. With a sure step and a fine-tuned ear, the beast ventures into Cuchimilcos.

****

In the village, Ollantay moves around with difficulty due to the number of obstacles he encounters while the anaconda explores the most hidden corners. In the face of adversity, the spirit's courage is redoubled and, finally, he stumbles upon a half-open door. Confident, he fixes his hands on the lock, which turns with the force of the winds. At intervals, Ollantay contemplates more than a dozen ceramic vases being dragged outside.

In his eagerness to continue with his task, the spirit attempts a risky move and receives a vase in the chest that rolls across the floor and drags him along. The vase ascends the steep paths leading up to the yellow-flowered cottage, straight towards the front door. The rolling object moves forward at such speed that Ollantay himself is unable to stop it and it crashes into the door, shattering into a thousand pieces. The spirit flies through the air and falls into Helébora's living room. Without hesitation, Ollantay throws the piece of cloth into the room and leaves without leaving any trace of his presence.

*****

At such a noise, Helébora leaves the bed in fear. Despite her fears, she goes to the living room to witness a horrifying spectacle: the front door has literally been destroyed and the scattered fragments of wood are fluttering in the wind. Filled with terror, she runs to hide under the covers next to her mother. But she is no longer there.

*****

The sensation of the proximity of a spirit unleashes the fury of the beast. In that home of yellow flowers, the diaphanous and luminous air points towards the living room, where the smells of the past that permeate it stand out. The feline eyes guide the anaconda to end its torments.

*****

Ollantay is alarmed by the conviction that it is unfair to end his existence in this way. He joins his hands and implores his god in the shadows to control his fear. The anaconda seems to follow the path marked by the feline eyes, unleashing a merciless fury and knocking down everything that crosses its path. Ollantay fears being discovered, but boldly manages to dodge the beast's gaze and disappear from the stage. His god had heard him, his god had helped him. And Ollantay gives thanks.

*****

"How strange..." murmurs the anaconda, "until a few moments ago the feline eyes were giving me alarming signals, and now everything is cloudy and uncertain. Perhaps I was alarmed for nothing."

After winding long roads, searching around every nook and cranny, he is relieved not to find a trace of the past. The anaconda resolves to stop no more in the Andes and concludes its visit to earth. It climbs hills and mountains, walks on the clouds and takes the road that leads directly to the domains of the Oracle. There he rushes to return the feline eyes.

"Now I leave safely, knowing for certain that the past was buried centuries ago. The men of today do not possess the watchword of the master of time."

"You affirm that nothing happened on earth with a certainty that truly baffles me," replies the Oracle.

"You'll see; you'll see... Time will prove me right."

*****

In the Inca huaca of Pacha Rurac, the kneeling spirits bid farewell to the earthly world before returning to their initial state. Up to that moment, everything has been terrible cries, sorrows and delusion. However, Ollantay has new hope. With a confident step, he advances towards Aucari to communicate the good news.

"Good news!" Ollantay shouts euphorically. The piece of cloth was placed long before the anaconda discovered it. We are saved!

The incredulous eyes turn to him as Ollantay rejoices. He repeats his words. Like a crazed child, he runs around the huaca in search of encouraging words, going round and round, dazed by so much agitation. He feels he deserves a reward. In his subconscious he already imagines himself riding on the back of a white llama, touring the most beautiful mountains of the Andes.

"Well? Thanks to my feat we can once again greet life."

"Yes, I agree that our stay on earth is not over yet," Aucari affirms. But I will not allow any one of you to contradict our mission, which is to populate Cuchimilcos with Inca descendants. From this moment on, I will not tolerate any stupidity.

After moments of anxiety, tranquility is restored in the huaca. The inhabitants of Pacha Rurac hold hands and thank their god for this new opportunity.

The Anaconda

The story goes that after the destruction of Pacha Rurac, the forces of evil, dissatisfied with the conquered territory and reneging on the promises made to the surrounding villages, decided to extend their dominion and strike the coup de grace against these people to also take over their lands and properties.

It all started with a number of relatively strange phenomena that followed one after the other. The sky indicated alarming signs, day and night. The horizon, dark as night, seemed to engulf the mountain peaks and from deep in the earth mysterious roars could be heard. Disoriented, llamas, alpacas, vicuñas and guanacos gathered at the foot of the mountains and repeatedly traveled the same route. A great flight of birds of all species fluttered over trees that were drying, bare and whose roots protruded from the ground. As soon as the sun's rays appeared in the east, dense black clouds hid them.

The Andean territory was transformed before the frightened eyes of its inhabitants.

The squalls announcing misfortune blew in the Andes singing mournful songs that penetrated the deepest part of the soul. And the musicians and poets, afflicted by this metamorphosis, toured the sacred mountains to implore the end of this nightmare with their chants and prayers.

In his grotto, Chacta listened to the sound of piercing gusts of wind, the roar of wild beasts and sad Andean melodies. Restless, he set off in search of his faithful friend Intillimay to witness the events. Hardly had he left his cave when he witnessed a terrible mutation. A display of stars descended from the firmament announcing the sad outcome. "What had happened?" he wondered in dismay as nature raged against the villagers.

He needed to know more and so he climbed Hanan Pupu, the highest snow-capped peak in the Andes. Once on the summit, he noticed a chilling fact: the destruction of Pacha Rurac. Distressed and disoriented, he could not find answers to his many questions; no matter how hard he tried to put his thoughts in order, he could hardly understand those sudden changes. The Andes were undergoing a profound transformation.

Grief-stricken, Chacta could not believe that a city as splendid as Pacha Rurac had disappeared from the face of the earth. That scenario was beyond unimaginable. His desire to know exactly what had happened intensified, and with that idea in mind he descended the mountain, stunned by the spectacle of the transformation. The matter was urgent: as time went by, the misfortune grew worse.

In his quest, his body became frostbitten as he beheld the disproportionate contours of a hideous figure emerging from the depths of the earth, rising amidst clouds and winds. It was a monster whose stature surpassed the mountaintops. The animal-headed giant bent down and, amid fires drawn from the crust of the earth, began a ceremonious ascent into the clouds. At last he could see it: it was a great lizard, whose colossal body was covered with tattoos. It poured a cup of burning flames on the earth.

Livid, Chacta had just realized that the Andes were entering a new era.

After a few hours of walking, he reached the outskirts of a city surrounded by a gigantic fire. Intillimay traced circles in the sky to show his friend the path to follow.

Clouds of dust and earth rose up to the sky; the wind, like an animal in fury, mercilessly tore away everything in its path. It was another time, another universe. Heart-rending cries of pain and weeping flooded the air.

Chacta, helpless, saw that everything was going badly without being able to control the situation. She needed to know more, to find out as soon as possible the origin of the damage.

Suddenly, a deafening blast was heard. A gigantic dust rose from a devilish whirlpool that cracked the earth, engulfing animals, men, women and children amidst a terrifying echo that repeated itself incessantly. Followed by a sinister and cavernous voice announcing the new kingdom.

"Poor mortals! It is useless to flee, your time has come!"

Chacta was convinced that the spirit of evil, son of fire, smoke, lightning and thunder had settled in the world, spreading its pestilent odor. In a short time the Andes were covered by a dark cloak such as had never been seen before. The gigantic lizard descended from the heavens, and evil took possession of the new kingdom.

Nothing to expect, no more miracles. The sinister process continued, the lizard sank deeper into the bowels of the earth and the neighboring villages of Pacha Rurac became its slaves. The beast lost its legs as it penetrated the earth, until it became a gigantic anaconda.

The air was filled with lamentations and complaints. Cities, towns and villages disappeared one after another, while the sorrowful moon wept the *Yawar Wek'e* ('tears of blood').

At Pacha Rurac, only one old tree was left standing: a centuries-old elm tree with gigantic branches. Since the arrival of the anaconda, the immense elm had undergone brutal transformations. The tree began to twist, shaken by a furious wind that tore the leaves from its branches, spitting out roots that crashed everywhere, committing outrages. The elm, which seemed to respond to a mean force, was the force of the beyond. Deeply convulsed, its roots moved to the rhythm of a deafening sound. In a short time, the elm succumbed under the yoke of the anaconda.

Under his orders, the tree became the guardian of the kingdom. A fervent follower of evil at whose disposal it gave its immense roots to facilitate the movements of the monster's army.

-Perfect! -the beast exclaimed triumphantly.

The anaconda then ordered his warriors to cling to the roots of the elm tree, which with frantic movements were cracking the earth.

It was in this climate of desolation and in this devastated region that the anaconda established its dominion. It reigned in the Andes from its subway palace, from where it would never leave.

Chacta could not escape the rapidly changing reality. All was lost. Accustomed to doing good on earth, he now felt responsible.

-How could I have allowed evil to take hold of the Andes?

Everything was slipping through his hands. Everything was falling apart. And he regretted not having intervened in time.

The wind finally stopped blowing and Chacta felt invisible forces taking possession of him, as if a diabolical beast was tugging at his feet. In an attempt to resist, he implored the sun god not to abandon him as he searched for something to hold on to and avoid the descent into the depths of the earth. Despite his increasingly anguished pleas, his demands were fruitless. Chacta was sucked into the heart of evil.

I was falling into an unknown world.

The thought of losing his friend terrified Intillimay, who, seeing him gradually disappear from the face of the earth, propelled himself with renewed energy into the air to come to his rescue. He descended fleetingly to where the Benefactor of the Andes was and stretched out his paws. Seeing the unconditional help his companion offered him, Chacta's hands clutched at the bird's legs, which lifted them both into the air. For an instant, he was freed from that hell on earth.

After a risky attempt to save his master, Intillimay the condor did his best to keep flying. However, he was aware that he could not support his weight for long. But they were still in the skies, and Chacta could observe the increasing destruction of the landscape.

He who had created the mountains, plains, rivers, streams, vegetation and placed living beings on the earth without forgetting any detail. The prayers of the inhabitants, their cries, spread throughout the Andes in demand of a divine intervention. Unanswered questions were raised to the sky. In those moments of intense feverishness, between complaints, laments and scenes of horror, the firmament was transformed into a vision of hope.

An opinion came down from the heavens, manifesting itself in the form of a luminous curtain that, when it cleared, revealed a vase, the one that had been used by the conglomerate of peoples to which Chacta was led blindfolded. The object was very particular, since it showed the design of a funerary mask in gold inlaid with precious stones. As Chacta contemplated it thoughtfully, the mask's eyes lit up, the lips opened and gave out a very important and non-transferable message.

Simultaneously, the events were precipitated. Intillimay, powerless after exhausting his resources, was descending rapidly due to the weight he was carrying. Seeing the difficulties Intillimay was facing, Chacta detached his legs to prevent the condor from collapsing. On his descent into the abyss, he witnessed something extraordinary.

The vase was tied to her neck with an alpaca wool filament mixed with gold fibers. When she touched it, Chacta felt that the air around it transmitted a hidden message among strange whispers. A connotation of prophecy.

Meanwhile, Intillimay did not give up. Despite the failure of his first attempt, he fought with stoicism and took flight again, evaluating alternatives to save his friend. Finally, he opted to throw a thick rope, but even that did not succeed. The murderous dust burned the rope without mercy.

After contemplating several failed attempts, Chacta realized that the efforts of his brave condor would be in vain.

"Intillimay, do not stay close to me. Despite your strength and fortitude, you could be the next victim of this hecatomb. You are the only one who could survive this tragedy. Go on, run away. That's an order, hurry. And remember that we will meet again."

The condor had the impression of leaving behind a part of himself. "How can I fly without the one with whom my beautiful mission is to do good on earth?" he thought. He had fought valiantly to save Chacta, but despite his efforts his friend was sinking little by little into a deep hole. With eyes wet with tears, the Benefactor of the Andes raised his gaze to his companion in adventure and expressed himself with great solemnity:

"I am a hopeless case, Intillimay. Don't try any harder. I ask you for my sake and for the sake of all these unfortunates who will soon fall to the bottom of the abyss. Go away! You will be more useful at liberty than as a prisoner at my side."

Chacta pointed to Hanan Pupu, the sacred mountain that from that moment on would be his refuge. Heartbroken, the condor wanted to respect the last will of his friend. Intillimay stopped struggling with the enormous crack in the earth that continued to drag Chacta with no escape. In his vertiginous fall, he watched in horror the multitude of people falling like him.

The Benefactor of the Andes was a kind of sage of the ancient world whose intuition had developed over the years. He received a divine intelligence that fortunately was not taken from him with the loss of his powers. He now judged the sordid world of which he was to become a part and formulated his own conclusions. The duty he had been entrusted with was to protect the prophecy of whoever was worthy in the air, and for this he needed to hide in a safe place the vase that hung from his neck.

He remembered the prophecy that the wind had whispered to him. The essence of its message referred to the missing link of the civilization of Pacha Rurac.

In the world born of destruction everything was advancing rapidly; the troops of the anaconda were positioned in the different corners of the kingdom, cornering their victims; men, women and children retreated in terror and pushed each other as they tried to flee. It was useless. Chacta let himself be dragged helplessly by that crowd that was so maddened by so much fear and pain. In the midst of the desperation of his people, he dropped the vase in a muddy field, where it was impossible to find it again among the human tide that prevented him from making his way to retrieve it. Bad luck. As fate would have it, the vase continued along the path that had been marked out for it.

After resigning himself to the loss of the valuable object, Chacta recognized some voices in the midst of the terrified crowd: they were the shamans of various nations who, full of remorse, implored the forgiveness of the Benefactor of the Andes. The latter asked them if they knew the origin of this cataclysm. But, believing them to be victims, he still had trouble understanding. On the verge of losing his mind, Chacta questioned a woman who was nearby. She was the one who, whimpering and stammering, revealed to him the events that had led to that moment.

It was at that moment that the Benefactor of the Andes understood his mistake. The closest shamans shunned him out of shame. Anger invaded Chacta, and the peaceful man who never exploded in anger addressed those shamans in these terms:

"You are like those snakes that proliferate in the earth!"

It was impossible to avoid all responsibility. Chacta had just realized that by helping them he was already part of the evil and had contributed to the destruction of the most beautiful place on earth: Pacha Rurac. He was the only one to blame for that tragedy that emptied the Andes of its inhabitants.

Terror seized Chacta when an abominable monster appeared, his face hidden behind a magnificent funerary mask. He was accompanied by an immense army of soldiers with grim faces, all dressed in long black tunics and tattoos of a snake on the right arm.

The terrible anaconda, that's what it was all about. It solemnly proclaimed the advent of its dominion.

"I welcome you to the Kingdom of Darkness, from which no one will emerge alive. Centuries will pass and you will remain my slaves; from today, you will do nothing but obey me. Otherwise, you will succumb atrociously."

Chacta could not conceive that what he was experiencing was true; seething with anger, he advanced towards the shamans.

"Do you realize what you have just done? I will tell you: thanks to you, we are destined to live with evil for eternity."

And the shamans kept asking for forgiveness. Forgiveness for their faults, for not having been sincere, forgiveness, forgiveness, forgiveness... Things could not go on like that.

As the Benefactor of the Andes, Chacta's duty was to prevent the towns and cities from falling under the yoke of the forces of evil. The moment was crucial and his participation decisive. Under no circumstances would he tolerate the loss of his freedom and that of the victims of that misfortune. To do so, he would have to make use of his supernatural powers. If he still had them.

To encourage his fellow sufferers, he told them:

"Do not lose faith, for there is still hope. I am Chacta, the Benefactor of the Andes."

Optimism reappeared in the hearts of the crowd, and the good news spread like a rolling snowball. It was an immense chain of unfortunate people placing their trust in one man.

In a short time, the crowd surrounded Chacta. In the midst of misfortune and desolation, an escape was being forged, the first from the Kingdom of Darkness. In spite of the fear that could be read on the faces of the men, the Andean settlers knew they were not alone. The Benefactor of the Andes was ready to guide those fallen in disgrace.

Chacta requested absolute silence, not on a whim, but as a kind of consolation that would communicate to him with illusion the possibility of reversing the situation in which they found themselves. Thus it was that, defying all power, he knelt down and raised his hands towards the sky.

He articulated his hands that had assisted him so much in a dance of gestural language. He turned them, advanced and retreated as if calling the sun god, imploring him to come to meet him. After a few attempts, his request proved fruitless, no change was produced and the energy of the sun, which on other occasions imbued him quickly, was not present.

Everything was clear, the warning of the Sun God hammered in his head, Chacta had misused his powers in that rite with the shamans of the villages surrounding Pacha Rurac and, therefore, he had lost his powers. Now the curse was upon him. "Why, why, why?" he repeated to himself without consolation. Guilt and helplessness formed a lump in his throat. He, who had fostered false hopes in the hearts of that desperate crowd, was incapable of getting them out of that horrible place alive.

With a serious gesture and a voice from beyond the grave, he announced his failure:

"Impossible. I cannot help you. My powers have left me."

The consternation was total. Chacta tried to conceal his discomfort, the feeling of not considering himself good for any-thing, but his gloom was palpable. Compressed, he moved away from the crowd to prostrate himself in a corner. It was unbelieva-ble that Chacta, the bearer of good who aspired to a better world and was burning with the desire to help, should suffer his first fall.

The anaconda boasted after seeing the unsuccessful attempt.

"I warn you not to try to flee my kingdom," he threatened sternly, "for if you do, you will be cruelly punished."

Chacta listened crestfallen as he discovered his new habitat: a bleak territory, full of rocks, swamps, labyrinths and tunnels crowded with people whose terrified faces turned to the Benefactor of the Andes, pleading and anxious for a solution. But he had suffered the wrath of the Sun God, as he had been warned the day he received his powers. Although involuntarily, he was responsible for the tragedy, since he had been the intermediary between the earth and the afterlife.

Now death was running through the Andes.

In the depths of the Kingdom of Darkness there was no dawn and no spring. Twilight reigned as a despot. Deprived of his gifts, the Benefactor of the Andes was a mere mortal. Suddenly, the voice of the anaconda brought them out of their meditation.

"I need men I can trust!"

The shamans of various nations, cowardly and hypocritical, rushed to swear allegiance to the monster for fear of enduring the worst atrocities. Chacta refused, which earned him a severe reprimand. The anaconda could have easily eliminated him, but there was a momentous obstacle: Chacta was the crucial piece to the success of the beast's plan. He was the only man who could be used as a symbol.

"In time this rebel will eventually submit," said the anaconda.

Under his reign, the Andes underwent unspeakable and terrible transformations. The anaconda, which had spent centuries without devouring the most insignificant of prey, made up for lost time by gobbling up its first victims. From the beginning of his supremacy, this terrible sovereign began a close and permanent surveillance of the land, preventing mortals attracted by the legend of Pacha Rurac, and especially by his riches, from discovering the Kingdom of Darkness.

He exterminated any intruder.

He had a very peculiar way of eliminating them: he would scatter jewels and valuables to attract greedy men thirsty for riches. Once captured, he wrapped them with the terrible rings of his tail, strangled them and threw them into one of the many abysses where they would discover the face of death.

For centuries, the anaconda was feared by all his vassals. He reigned as a tyrant, possessed great wealth and inordinate strength.

In this ocean of misfortune, the former inhabitants of the regions engulfed by the catastrophe became his subjects, forced to blindly obey his will. Confined in cells, they lived in darkness. However, not everything was dark in the Kingdom of Darkness,

the anaconda also knew how to show herself generous, satis-
fying her slaves on some occasions with lavish feasts in which
she paraded with her innumerable cloaks and masks. During the
festive days, the meals were copious; the music, omnipresent; and
the slaves forgot for a moment their sadness, the vexations and
the aggressions that they endured daily.

As for Chacta, the Benefactor of the Andes, the destruction
of Pacha Rurac was the greatest burden on his conscience.
Throughout his life, his mission had been to do good on earth
and, through an error of judgment, he now found himself
dispossessed of his gift, leaving evil to triumph in the Andes.

Helébora in Torment

After the events of the previous night, Cuchimilcos wakes up to a calm morning. Those terrible winds have devastated much of the town like a horde of barbarians. Fortunata comes out of hiding to see that the main gate of the house is scattered on the ground.

"I would swear that a battle of savages has been waged at the entrance to our house, my daughter."

Descending slowly down the steep path of the village, Fortunata realizes that she is not the only one affected. She runs to the altarpiece, where an unusual discovery makes her skin crawl: the earth has been completely removed.

"Has someone moved the earth unceremoniously? Or maybe... something?"

"But where did you hide yesterday, Mom? I remember we hugged each other tightly as soon as the movements started. Later I covered myself with the sheets, but then I left for a moment to see what was going on in the living room, and when I came back, you were no longer in bed."

"I was so, so afraid that I hid under the bed," confesses the mother. It seemed to me the safest place in those circumstances."

"For a moment I was so scared that I ran to open the door of the house to look for help, but the force of the winds made me desist. We're lucky we only have to repair one door, look at the other houses and all those trees uprooted!"

"So many strange phenomena... First, that earth tremor; then, the trees like specters on the road. I would say that tonight we have been attacked by giants from the past."

"It's still too early to speculate," says Helébora. "Let's wait to discuss it with the rest of the town."

"What terrifies me, daughter, is that these massive trees were planted in the time of the Incas and were our protection. Now they have been uprooted by those merciless winds."

"I, too, have had some disturbing experiences lately. For example..."

A revelation slowly emerges from his lips, but at the first word the spirits seal his mouth.

"Be careful not to divulge our secrets, Helebora," they say.

Visibly stunned, the young woman chooses to remain silent.

"You were saying, daughter?"

"No, it's nothing. Forget about it."

Everything is so confusing that it makes no sense. Overwhelmed by so much destruction, Helébora and her mother go down to Don Gumersindo's house, who is already waiting for them outside, clearly convulsed by what has happened.

For a moment, Helébora has the feeling that the eyes of all the inhabitants are fixed on her. Embarrassed, she warns her mother to go home, convinced that the facts are conclusive. So, in a fit of anger, she throws the dolls to the ground. When Fortunata returns, she decides to take her daughter away from the Inca vases before the young girl loses her sanity.

"Do not mistreat what has cost you so much effort. The day you want to work on the dolls again, you will take them out of the Inca vases."

"Mom, I'm scared. I think I have gone too far with this idea of searching the past. I am sure that with my act I have revived mysterious forces beyond my control."

"I don't know what to tell you, daughter."

"I think I should give up participating in the fair. The night we have just suffered is only the prelude to our destruction."

"Things will fall under their own weight. Try to show sanity and don't get carried away by beliefs."

Mixed up in a labyrinth of contradictions, Helébora does not realize that her rejection of the dolls' project causes her to sink little by little into darkness. Her raison d'être fades away as her subconscious is poisoned by the stubborn idea that there is a curse. His sixth sense warns him that the dolls are cruel, merciless, murderous... to the point that they will wipe out the town. Under the pretext of avoiding a misfortune, he covers up his shame of having enrolled in the artisan competition, transforming his life into a monotonous list of repetitive acts.

The days go by and Helébora continues with this idea: "Dolls are no good". This lethargic state unsettles her. In recent times, she lives in torment. She needs to confide in her only friend, so she picks up a scouring pad and sets off to meet him. As she cautiously descends, she notices that the earth on the path is soft and a dense air impregnated with the smell of dry grass pervades everything. Suddenly, huge stones roll down in the vicinity.

"I must be careful not to fall."

In her confusion, she gives way so that the gigantic stones continue down the hillside. Helébora loses her strength as she approaches Don Gumersindo's house. Gumersindo welcomes her with a glass of water.

"What's the matter, my daughter? Express yourself."

"It's nothing, just a couple of rocks that were harassing me. It's all over now, forget it. The important thing is that I'm here with you."

"Is something wrong? Tell me. How can I help you?"

"I just came to talk. I don't know what to do anymore and I need your advice."

"Relax, Helébora. I'll make you some tila tea and we'll sip it together. Relax."

"Lately, I have been thinking a lot and I have come to the conclusion that all the phenomena I have experienced are the product of my curiosity. Hidden secrets that held thousands of messages have been put on earth, exposing them to this earthly world. And because of this there are evil spirits that will condemn Cuchimilcos and the young woman who dared to reveal them."

"No, Helébora. Get that crazy idea out of your mind. The whole town has witnessed these earth and air movements. Do not blame yourself. Neither you nor your dolls are the cause of such acts. Always remember that the dead are dust and dust they will remain. They do not have the power to revive and, above all, they have never come to disturb the living. The dolls are magical, but in no book is there any mention of black magic, on the contrary: they have protected thousands of souls in the past. Don't go on accusing yourself and leave things as they are. Remember that nature is governed by chance."

"Listen to this, Don Gumersindo! The pieces of cloth that I kept in my room, where no one could touch them, changed places on the day of the tragedy. Now they are inside the Inca vases. Faced with the unusualness of the situation, I was blinded by anger and threw some dolls on the floor."

"Daughter, I am going to ask you not to try to find a logical explanation for events beyond our control. I can't go any further in my reasoning, so the only advice I give you is to look inside yourself for that breath of authenticity that we all have. Do it, when your heart asks for it."

Don Gumersindo's comforting words reassure Helébora. On her way home, she carefully examines the dolls and observes them in silence, determining that there is nothing pleasant about them. Lost in thought, she imagines that those pieces of cloth have a dark soul like her face.

The days of monotony are counted like flocks. But during a lovely evening, a neighbor intercepts her mother on her way home.

"Go down to the market quickly, Doña Fortunata. Very important news awaits you."

Running with her basket in hand, the mother does not stop, despite the effort, until she reaches the enclosure where the announcement awaits her. Making her way through the crowd, she manages to position herself among the first and arrives in time to hear such an important message.

"Listen up, Andean artisans, we're looking for you! Finally, the time has come to showcase your talents at the Picha Fair. Don't miss this opportunity and introduce yourselves."

"This news is for my daughter," says Fortunata. I have to go tell her.

The mother finds Helébora in the mountains during her daily walk with the llamas. The young woman's heart is turned upside down when she learns that she still has time to sign up for the Picha Fair. Excitement invades her, the challenge transforms her, and she renounces her fear when the desire for the confection awakens. But how does she know that dolls do not cause evil?

Helébora wanders day and night near the Inca vases, disguising her presence with an inordinate cleaning of the house as she watches them for evidence of her evil deeds. From dust to grease, from changing the flowers to washing the vases, the menial tasks are repeated countless times. After a few weeks of repetitive chores, she recognizes that perhaps she has overdone it and those dolls are just angels in patchwork disguises whose harmless faces exude security when viewed. Immediately, the urge to take up the confection again takes hold of her heart.

"I have probably disfigured reality. How could I have been so blind? My dolls are harmless."

With the same wildness with which she threw the dolls on the floor and abandoned her work, she now resumes her work with an inordinate eagerness. She places the fabrics, scissors, needles, threads and molds on the table. Hidden in their secret hiding place, the spirits are attracted by the new vibrations and awaken from their slumber. These are times of change. Times of joy. At last the abandoned work is resumed. The spirits intertwine their hands and make their way to the little yellow house.

In the town of Cuchimilcos, a delirious rattling sound is heard in the air. The inhabitants look at each other in confusion, trying to identify the origin of the sound. It is the spirits, who have raised an immense dust that prevents the inhabitants from moving freely through the streets of their town. They overflow roads and stretches, taking shortcuts to reach their destination.

Once at Helébora's home, creativity is manifested at its best. With tests of dexterity, the spirits infiltrate the profound wisdom of the affairs of ancient times into the young woman's memory, so that no one doubts the skill of her creators. Diaphanous images circulate the room. When they take a piece they make up for lost time with magnificent execution. The spirits are excited and get down to work. And this time Aucari will not allow any more foolish acts.

"It's nice to feel invisible," the spirits murmur.

Ollantay relives a lost dream. He moves away from his own and in the corner of the ceiling he raises and lowers fabrics to show his favorite ones.

"Ollantay, listen and obey. That's not how I want it," shouts Aucari in displeasure. It will be with gentleness and patience that we will obtain good results. Now you may go, for I will not allow you to sabotage the work.

Undaunted by such a reaction, Ollantay chooses to walk away. He blends into the melee as he feels he has been displaced, so his ego suffers. Meanwhile, the group shouts in chorus.

"Let him go! Yes! Let that daring apprentice go!"

Once the hindrance has disappeared, the teachers at each end of the table receive the instructions that their boss dictates to them.

"The work has to be impeccable, and don't forget to add the protective puff to each copy."

Helébora's hands are guided by experts in the field during stitching. One scissor after another ends the molds while the frayed fabrics are cleaned without hesitation.

The air becomes cooler and to prevent Helébora from losing concentration Aucari orders the master of the crystal to force the enclosure, preventing the hours of shade from penetrating the room. The young woman would not feel the fatigue and the light will remain until the work is finished. The crystal master, knowing beforehand his experiences, employs thousands of objects to maintain the balance between day, night and light. For the first time, the room must remain lit until the last piece of confection. Dazed and lacking appetite, the crystal master devotes himself day and night to carry out the task. Night falls and he continues between sketches and doodles.

"What you demand of me is an ordeal," he says to the curaca.

"Do you realize that with your act we will save an entire civilization?" Aucari replies. Then she looks around. The room is very dark.

Suddenly, the crystal master remembers that in ancient times coca leaves kept him awake at night. With great leaps he sets off into the woods, where he deftly plucks the best specimens from the coca fields. They are counted by the hundreds, each one more beautiful than the last, and the crystal master takes them to the room, where he nails them to the walls and ceilings.

"Give a quick rotation," he says to the curaca, "because in a short time you will find the light."

The master of the crystal opens the windows and the luminous insects come to the call, making deep hissing sounds. In a few seconds they completely invade the room.

Helébora is delighted and never ceases to thank Divine Providence.

"The scent of the countryside is in this room."

The murmur of approval among his people makes it easier for the crystal master to complete his work. But the work continues. The darning progresses under the light of the insects and the promise of the crystal master: the work will continue through the night.

The anaconda perceives the coca inhalations, which incite it to sleep and lower its guard.

After several days of tireless tailoring, Fortunata enters the room, where she finds Helébora raving.

"What's the matter? Do you have something, my daughter?"

"I've never felt so good in my life as I do now, Mom. Making these dolls is amazing. They create, cut and sew themselves. Sometimes I feel like I have company."

"Anything is possible in these ancestral lands. The inhabitants of Cuchimilcos are convinced that not far from here a majestic civilization succumbed and devoted itself to doing good. They protect us. However, other beliefs tell us that evil spirits destroyed it all, from flesh to bone. I hope the latter are not among us."

"Don't worry, Mom. We have the good vibes."

Seduced by the interest of presenting herself to the competition, Helébora stays up all night. Hundreds of dolls are produced, each one more special. To the rhythm of scissors, embroidery and finishing, the young woman keeps the dream alive.

"My path is laid out. Now all that remains is to finish the dresses."

Her intuition has not betrayed her, and she dedicates herself to the task with redoubled effort and perseverance. Veils. Ornaments. Belts. Accessories. When she finishes, joy shines on her face, a joy that fills her with satisfaction after a job well done. With a smile on her lips, Helébora announces the end of the work and signs up for the Picha Fair.

A few days of enthusiasm pass, which Helébora fills with the hustle and bustle of everyday life, prolonged visits to her friend Don Gumersindo and tending to the flames. She anxiously awaits the outcome.

On a very rare evening, with the reddish sky covering the mountains, Fortunata opens the door of her home to the letter carrier.

"I have traveled all over the world to get to this house," says the man. "Does Helébora Rumi live here?"

"Yes, this is your home."

"This letter is for her. Sign here, please. -Hearing the last sentence, Fortunata blushes. Madam, are you feeling well?" asks the letter carrier. "Just sign here, please."

"I don't know how to sign," confesses the woman in a half-voice.

"Do you know the sign of the cross?"

"Yes, sir."

"Then make a cross."

Half hidden by the door, Fortunata draws the cross as best she can. When the letter carrier leaves, the mother, letter in hand, sets off in search of Helébora. Flying over the prairies and along dangerous paths, between whistles that sound like shrieks, Fortunata communicates the good news to her daughter.

"What's the matter, Mom?" asks Helébora with curiosity when she sees her mother's eyes, reddened by crying. "What's all the fuss about?"

"My daughter, my daughter, I have received your letter of acceptance!"

Helébora can't believe that the competition finally has a date. Days of insomnia come as the big day approaches. Her mind is filled with bad thoughts and her confidence leaves her. The girl paces up and down the house in search of inspiration.

"Stop worrying, my daughter. Your work speaks for itself."

In between the wit and nonsense, Helébora prepares her exhibition, frightened by the possibility of a horrendous disqualification. She rambles as she selects some samples for the judges. Looking at them carefully one by one, she begs not to make a mistake while imploring God. Hearing the prayers, the spirits awaken a bit groggy, but move on without qualms. Helébora needs them. They leave the huaca, fly over the village and enter the little house with the yellow flowers. The long-awaited moment has finally arrived.

"Take it, my daughter," says Fortunata, handing her a gunny sack. May luck be with you.

Helébora approaches her mother with glassy eyes and hugs her tightly. Without saying anything else, she walks down the decayed road. As she walks away from her little house, she carefully descends to the house of Don Gumersindo, who is waiting for her with a cup of tila tea.

"This will do you good, girl. Come in for a few minutes, you look nervous."

"That's right, Don Gumersindo. The selection frightens me."

"I am convinced that your talent will be rewarded."

"Thank you, Mr. Gumersindo. Thank you very much for your unconditional support."

For a moment, between the smoke and the aroma of tea, the wise man tenderly remembers the day when Helébora, still a little girl, did the impossible to take him to the village healer. She is the apple of his eye, his spoiled child, and his love for her was one of those firm and permanent ones, and he shows it to her whenever he can with those little insignificant details that sometimes disarm her.

"Remember, Helébora, that since you were a child you have been stubborn and stubborn, and you have always achieved what you set out to do. Be sure that you will be chosen."

"Do you think so, Don Gumersindo?"

"I don't believe it, my daughter, your eyes confirm it to me. I see in them that overwhelming flame that characterizes you. You will be chosen. Now go, I don't want you to be late because of me."

Squeezing her tightly, Don Gumersindo wishes her luck. Stealthily, Helébora descends the slope while the spirits follow her in a procession. But the young woman stops in the middle of the path, observing the flames, the houses of her village and the familiar dust.

"This competition is not for me! -he says to himself. It's obvious that I'm going to make a fool of myself. I'd better go home."

Faced with such indecision, the spirits form a circle around Helébora. And Aucari and his people give her the necessary courage. She, who does not understand such designs, comes to the conclusion that both her mother and Don Gumersindo are right.

The Selection

It is early morning and a morning mist is spreading over the vast town of Picha. Restless, Helébora turns her head at every corner with an air full of curiosity, advancing towards the long-awaited event. But a terribly desolate sight fills her with dread. Wasteland streets welcome her in that land where she is used to know the commotion and bustle of a public thirsty for novelties that crowds together amidst laughter, noise and contagious dances.

But at that moment an eerie silence reigns. Helébora grips the sack of dolls tightly and walks towards the parks with a lost look in her eyes. The young woman pales when she realizes that a few steps away, as she calls it, the final judgment awaits her. The difficulty of the competition makes Helébora hesitate once again and questions her skill and creativity. She turns back to Cuchimilcos.

But startling revelations make him realize that nothing is lost. With this new resolve, he feels he is on the verge of an extraordinary feat. Despite the rigors of the weather, an anxious crowd waits in front of the gate where the selection will be held. A tall, upright man, with a dark complexion and eyes full of kindness, sees her arrive. He is in charge of opening the gates to start such a distinguished event. The inhabitants of Picha have poured into the enclosure where perfection and creativity will be the winners. Hearing the thunderous applause, Helébora is intoxicated by a feeling of superiority while the spirits encourage her with dreamy eyes.

-There is no worse defeat than that which is abandoned," they whisper in his ear, "and no worse battle than that which is not fought.

Comforted, Helébora hands over her letter of acceptance and enters the room. The man at the door tells her that she is the first to introduce herself. Helébora blushes as she notices the start time.

"What's the matter, young lady?"

"I wouldn't want to pass before everyone else. Actually, it's my first time and I'm trembling with fear."

"That happens very often. You'd better take it easy, otherwise you won't get very far. Where do you come from?"

"From Cuchimilcos, sir."

"Cuchimilcos! Did you say it right? -Cuchimilcos?"

"Yes, sir."

"The town of a thousand faces. Cuchimilcos is far away. No, you can't go back yet. Look, take this chair and place yourself near that curtain, from there you will see all the participants and you will introduce yourself when you feel better."

"Thank you, sir. I really don't know how to thank you."

As soon as Helébora calms down, Aucari organizes the spirits while keeping an eye on Ollantay, as if he wanted to blame him for something, and addresses his own.

"So far so good," Aucari explains. Come on, come in quickly. I want you all inside with the exception of Ollantay and Kero.

"Me?" replied Ollantay incredulously.

"Yes, you! I wouldn't want you to commit another imprudence. You two will remain at the entrance as guards. As soon as you see anything strange, let us know."

"All right," says Ollantay, disappointed.

Meanwhile, Helébora continues to lean on the arm of the chair, a spectator of a beauty she never imagined she would behold. Throughout the day the artisans arrive one by one to exhibit their work. Don Mamerto Huarcaya makes his way through the crowd, accompanied by thunderous applause and the long ovation of an anxious public. Fascinated, Helébora smiles without looking away in admiration. Don Mamerto, positioned in the center of the amphitheater, naturally offers a sample of his figures to each of the six judges. He is the master of masters, so a brief conversation is enough for him to be tacitly accepted.

During a handshake with don Mamerto, one of the jurors notices an unusual shadow. Upon closer inspection, he notices that it is a girl. Seeing him so agitated, the other judges stand up and ask him what the problem is. But he storms off towards the entrance.

"Chucho, can you explain to me what this girl is doing in the living room?"

"It's the first time she has presented herself. I saw her so insecure that to reassure her I offered her to sit over there, without disturbing the selection."

"You know very well that the regulations prohibit it."

"Yes, I know. But I couldn't tell him to go back home and come back later. We are talking about long distances: Cuchimilcos, to be more exact."

"Now I understand, Cuchimilcos is far away. I'll overlook it this time, but let it be the first and last time you don't abide by the rules. Otherwise, you will be fired."

"I understand, Your Honor."

Listening to the discussion, Helébora lowered her face in shame. The favor she has been granted is not correct and the judge has pointed it out. With her legs crossed and pressing her wrists tightly against her chest, the girl hides behind the curtain, for she wants nothing more than to avoid her gaze meeting that of the angry judge.

"What's going on?" ask the other jurors.

"This bold one has slipped in," explains the judge. "Look at her, she's sitting there."

"Who is it? Is it a new participant?"

"Yes, apparently she lives in Cuchimilcos and can't come and go again." Chucho offered her a chair in a corner of the room. "Let's go on, I don't want to make my life any more difficult."

The selection resumes with an imposing woman with a huge figure. She is Hermelinda Tapia, the artist of sculpted portraits. Using clay, she impresses with her skillful hands, a touch here and a touch there until in a short time the work is finished. In an instant, she sculpts the portrait of one of the gentlemen present. The judges are surprised and pleased by the speed and dexterity Hermelinda demonstrates with her hands. She is accepted and when she leaves, it is the turn of don Atilio Huamán, who uses bread crumbs to reproduce the flora and fauna of the Andes.

"Your work seems very complex," says one of the judges. "I need a sample of your skill."

Don Atilio uses a fine silk to dry his thick, rough fingers bordered with long fingernails. Then he attacks a piece of white and filthy dough that he takes out of a paper sack. Stirring a self-prepared liquid, made from a secret recipe, he spreads it on his fingers with which he rubs the dough. His long fingernails cut the material into several pieces, then he polishes them and models the silhouettes, taking the size of his fingernails as a measure for the faces and hats. Don Atilio represents a shepherd with his llamas. The judges, impressed by the many details, praise his work and the artist is accepted.

Meanwhile, in a corner of the enclosure, Helébora observes the strong performances of her competitors, nervous and dazed she is in full reflection, asking herself incessantly why she is there, how to continue with such a challenge? Unaware of all this world full of perfection, driven by contradictory feelings and with no more strength to continue, her only option is to flee, she repeats to herself incessantly. Meanwhile, the selection continues with one of Picha's most celebrated artists, don Hilario Mamani, creator of the saints and virgins with long necks. This year *The Last Supper* will be on display. Pleased, the judges greet him with much respect and flattery until they finally give their approval.

After the last selection, the venue empties. What was at first a display of creativity and skill that took memories and melted them onto the walls now fills with stillness as the selection for the Picha Fair closes.

In a chair in the corner, the girl of unknown name remains as a shadow. Nervous and exhausted by so much tension, Helébora lowers her head so as not to be seen, meditating on her fate, when an imperious voice calls out to her.

"Hey, you! Girl! The one hiding behind that curtain. You're the last of this test. Go ahead, we're about to close.

It is an implacable and cruel voice, accompanied by a look of rage and Helébora is frightened. Overwhelmed by her sorrows, the young girl only wants to flee from those unfriendly faces that do not inspire confidence in her. Faced with her indecision, the spirits inject her with the courage to continue.

"Go ahead, Helébora. You are already in the final stage. You can't give up now."

With a slow gait, she tries futilely to prepare to explain her proposal.

"Who sponsored you, girl?" asks a judge.

"Restless hands," the spirits whisper to Helébora.

"Restless hands?" she says.

"What nonsense! Let's not waste any more time," says another. "Come on, present your work."

Faced with the torture and censure of these men, Helébora places her samples on the table. One for each judge.

"What insolence is this? How dare you show up with such work?"

"I need more details," says another. "Go on, explain to us the reason for your audacity."

"Leave it! Her arguments will be banal."

One of the judges loses his patience with this contestant, gets up from his chair and slams one of his wrists against the wall. The spirits are scandalized by such a reaction. Another of the judges calls the young woman a witch while placing a crucifix in front of the dolls. Hearing the shouts and insults of the judges, Helébora covers her ears and her lips are sealed. She remains motionless.

"Go on, get out of here," says a judge, "and don't waste any more of our time."

"These rag dolls are worthless. The selection is finished."

In the meantime, the restless spirits review again and again the speech that Helébora is going to present.

"Spirit poet, now it will be your turn to direct this young lady," Aucari affirms. "Hurry up! Whisper what she should say in her ear."

The obedient spirit approaches and whispers his poem:

> In the fields of Cuchimilcos,
> tradition revived;
> on the lips of a young woman,
> the truth shone through.
> Several times melted in the darkness,
> my heart was lost,

walking like a soul in pain,
his reason found.
I am Helébora Rumi, whom you rejected,
but his dirty and merciless hand
will remember your bad deed.

The judges whisper among themselves. Paralyzed by bitterness and rage at what they had just heard, they stand up and arrange the chairs, ready to leave the room.

"We cannot disrespect the judges like this!" Aucari replied indignantly. "You are wrong, spirit poet. Your stupidity has gotten us into trouble."

-Yes, I take issue with the way they've treated Helebora and the dolls," replies the spirit poet.

But again he approaches the young woman and whispers to her what to recite:

Several times I wondered
the reason for my presentation,
and I answered myself:
Helébora, strengthen your tradition.
The day I discovered it
my heart pounded,
my ancestors are divine,
his legacy convinced me.
Long before the Incas ruled the world, the
our most precious riches,
Chancay dolls guarded by
the lives of the inhabitants,
now you, with your cowardice,
will prevent them from being protected.

Despite her boldness, the judges do not accept Helébora. What a disappointment!

She picks up her wrists from the floor. All seems lost, but, just as she prepares to leave, the two spirits at the entrance of the enclosure begin a tumultuous dispute.

"Today will be the big day," Ollantay affirms. "Helébora will convince the judges to allow her to participate in the Picha Fair if she presents a replica of an original doll. You know, while she was choosing the samples, I exchanged one of the dolls for another identical to the one I had, which was itself an imitation of the original doll."

"Stop talking nonsense," Kero interjects. "As far as I know, no one has seen the original doll. It was torn from the hands of Crown Prince Chancay."

"You are mistaken. I was present in the bedroom of the little prince, before his death, with my friend the priest of Chancay. There I met his father the Patriarch and I saw the original Chancay doll prostrate at the side of the little prince."

"Comparing his doll to the original is terrible," Kero thinks. "How presumptuous... Who does he think he is, the prodigy of the universe? This wretch has gone beyond the limits of respect, to talk so freely about that prodigious doll, possessed of supernatural powers... by what right?". His face reddened with anger, uncontainable anger, and, hurling words saturated with insults, he put an end to this absurd conversation.

"Poor fool, shut up. I'm tired of hearing your nonsense."

The remark is said with such a contemptuous tone that it causes a dent; his honor has been touched and Ollantay feels hurt. Terribly affected by these aggressions, he gives in to an impulsive reaction and his explosive character is boiling over. He opts for confrontation. Ollantay mechanically rubs his hands together to warm up before retorting in exasperation:

"What are you insinuating? That I am a liar? You know very well that I guided Helébora with an expert hand during the making of a doll which, by the way, is identical to the original."

"Oh yes, as if I were sucking my thumb. And now you will say that thanks to that reply Helébora will be accepted, eh? Well, as soon as we get to the Inca huaca I will tell the others that we have returned to earth for nothing. You alone hold the key to our past. With the original doll in hand, good will prevail in the Andes, won't it?"

Kero's tone is mocking. In response to such behavior, Ollantay's blushes and his blood boils with anger. Outraged by the affront, he tells himself that this incident is very serious and the only possible way is to respond by fighting. He stands in a considerable space in the light provided by the open gate of the enclosure and stretches out his gnarled fingers. Encouraged by the thought of delivering a beating to Kero that he will remember all his life, he flies around the spirit and shows him his fists, goading him to fight. He keeps constantly moving his feet to let him know that he is not a novice, but that he is capable of dodging any blow or wringing his neck if necessary.

"Come on, coward!" Ollantay exclaims, "Defend yourself before I smash your lying face!"

The tone of voice rises, and Kero, out of his mind, forgets Aucari's slogans and responds to his rival with violence. He leaps into the air and grabs the gate to close it on Ollantay's head. Ollantay resists and his skeletal body prevents the gate from moving an inch. Their bodies stretch, slip silently, their robes float through the air and move, exposing their legs. In a matter of seconds, the atmosphere is invaded by a myriad of inexplicable events, suspended, invisible movements, very small voices of a possible dispute accompanied by that pull and tug of the gate.

Chucho tries by all means to keep him in his place.

"What's going on here? This gate is moving by itself!"

His lost gaze, full of horror, slips through the entrance, through the corners, through the long corridor of the enclosure without finding the promoter of such an act. Trying to flee is impossible, because everything is happening so fast. He feels the thick hairs of his head stand up in fear that the sudden movements of the door may cause an accident and he decides to take refuge in a corner.

"Come on, defend yourself, you coward! " Ollantay repeats out of control. "Defend yourself if you don't want me to break your face with my fist."

"How strange!" says the doorman to himself, full of fear. "I hear some voices, as if someone was fighting, but... what's going on here? I don't see anyone."

Chucho doesn't believe what he hears and blames his imagination.

The opponents slap and punch each other in the air. Ollantay leans on Chucho to dodge them, and the goalkeeper's shirt is unbuttoned. His hair is pulled at both ends, the belt of his pants is released and his hat is thrown to the floor. Chucho's attempts to close the gate are in vain.

Something terrible is about to explode. Ollantay's ego has been wounded and he feels the imperious desire to emerge victorious from this encounter. Resolutely, looking sideways at the ceiling and breaking the respect of those present, Ollantay boasts of being the maker of fire and water. In his eagerness to punish his tough opponent, he employs a new tactic: he soars to the ceiling initiating disastrous movements, twists and turns with alarming speed and traces circles of air leaving Kero in a trance. Helpless, the other spirit allows itself to be dragged by this unforeseen whirlpool, so difficult to stop. Ollantay corners his rival.

Fists, kicks, heated screams..., everything is mixed together, sweeping away whoever crosses their path. With Kero's movements, the whirlwind that Ollantay has formed doubles in strength and speed, and in the face of such a disproportionate magnitude it is difficult to stop them.

In the passageway adjoining the room where the selection of participants for the Picha Fair is being concluded, vases, vases and curtains are violently torn and thrown. In a test of strength between the two spirits, the gate comes off and explodes as if it were made of glass.

Meanwhile, in the selection room, the disgruntled judges are finishing the selection when, suddenly, they are surprised by something incomprehensible: the thunderous noise of the door reaches their ears, accompanied by a violent cold air. The judges recoil in fear as they realize that this horrible phenomenon is advancing unmistakably towards them.

"What's going on here?" ask the judges, somewhat convulsed.

A voice from beyond the grave, the voice of the spirit poet, answers them:

"Accomplish your mission."

"Who is talking to me?" asks a member of the jury. "I don't understand anything."

The whirlpool continues its journey through the long passageway and makes its way to the selection room. Faced with such a strange situation, the judges fall silent. Thus, their wild eyes meet with the girl from Cuchimilcos. At that moment they realize that they have not finished with the selection and hurry to take their places.

"It's not the dolls that bring me here," says Helébora, "but the whole world. Please, you have to listen to me. These are protective dolls, made to help those in need."

The unheard of happens and the judges are petrified in their seats, which seem to sink under their weight. The lifeless dolls soar through the air and seem to ask to be accepted. Helébora advances with her tangled hair through the destructive air. Her veil and accessories follow the precise movements dictated by the situation. The dolls fall to the ground and then take flight again. Terrible shaking is heard and the dolls' hair flutters. The judges, unhinged and pale, murmur:

"Sir, where are those winds coming from?"

"It is terrible. A terrible nightmare."

Aucari is worried. Unaware of what is going on, he has the unpleasant impression that the origin of this disorder comes from his own people.

"They are Ollantay and Kero," explained a spirit. Look at them in the swirling wind.

"These idiots... I don't understand what's in their heads."

"I hear whispers all the time!" exclaims one of the judges. I think I'm going crazy.

"Let's get out of here before we lose our minds!" proposes another.

But when the judges get up to march, their wrists block their way. Whipped by these violent winds, the judges struggle to avoid being projected against the wall. One of the judges wishes he had magic shoes to escape from that place. The objects in the room break one by one while Helébora continues to show her dolls: the details of the making, the material used, the finishes... She expresses herself as a renowned seamstress.

The room is shaken from top to bottom, the dust that for years has accumulated in corners, ceilings, furniture and mirrors is diluted in the atmosphere. Amidst all the confusion, Aucari orders ten of her spirits to separate the two whippersnappers. But after a few seconds, the destruction is accentuated.

"This is more than my heart can bear," says a judge. "It's about to burst with fright."

"This girl has come from the high Andean mountains, from the village of Cuchimilcos," said one of the judges to reassure another.

"From where?"

"Cuchimilcos. Chucho she told me."

"Did you say Cuchimilcos?" The other nods. "Cuchimilcos is the cursed town of the Andes. Many stories run around here about that place. Some say its inhabitants are possessed by evil spirits, but I never imagined I'd meet an artisan from Cuchimilcos."

"Now I understand. This girl is angry and wants to punish us for all the insults we have subjected her to. We have to give her a chance if we want to get out of this place alive."

"Yes, this contestant is a real enigma that is difficult to decipher," concludes one of the judges. What do we do?"

Everything is more complex than it appears, and the judges are certain that something terrible will happen if they do not accept this artisan from Cuchimilcos.

"Young lady," the jury foreman says politely, "Do you have a statement to make?"

Helébora advances through the mess and respectfully explains how the dolls came into her life, and the reason for her mission. Her lips, gestures and attitude are at the height of the situation, her words dazzle and the audience outside, impressed by so much noise, listens to Helébora's speech with attention. Meanwhile, she continues with her explanation.

"If I understood the young lady correctly," murmurs one of the judges, "these dolls have souls."

"Let's avoid unleashing the wrath of the Andes. Let's put an end to this candidate once and for all."

The judges, at the limit of their sanity, agree to Helébora's work.

"These dolls have life and charm," says a judge to the young woman. You have convinced us. You are accepted. The Picha Fair will begin in three weeks. We wish you the best of luck. And now, if you will excuse us, we have to leave.

What a joy! She has been accepted. Helébora cannot believe it. All is merriment and the audience is cheering and clapping. The spirits, more than happy, dance on one foot, the women spirits hold hands while they twirl around and Kero and Ollantay, exhausted, give up their fight. Aucari reprimands them harshly for their unprecedented behavior and the two spirits bow their heads, fearful of punishment.

Once she returns to the little house of yellow flowers, Helébora tells her mother what happened in detail. Proudly, Fortunata gives her daughter the necklace of her ancestors.

"For many centuries, this necklace was passed down from generation to generation. Now it is your responsibility to preserve it. You will give it to your firstborn daughter as soon as you see her interest in preserving what is ours, so that she will do the same with her daughter and thus continue the tradition."

As soon as it is placed around her neck, the mask that adorns the necklace lights up her golden eyes for an instant. Helébora, oblivious to this, accepts it gladly. She still reflects on how she has been able to overcome her fears and gather the courage to conquer the judges and gain acceptance at the Picha Fair.

The Announcement

In the Kingdom of Darkness, Chacta, the Benefactor of the Andes, was suffocating in that labyrinth with no way out. His innate desire to do good had been limited. The pain and misfortune of his people was constantly running through the opaque walls of the kingdom, inciting him to rebel. And Chacta was punished for disobeying the orders given by the guards of the anaconda.

Often he would go inside, lamp in hand, on his evening pilgrimage. He melted into the cracked and deformed labyrinths, leaving only his footprints as the only testimony. He hardly showed himself at the threshold of the cells, his presence was welcomed by the prisoners. Chacta silenced the sorrows with a quick intervention and instilled a will to live in the numerous families that for centuries had lived buried in those prisons. Chacta had the ability to listen and understand the problems that afflicted people and, after hours of unburdening, he would offer them his wise advice.

Dominated by the precept of helping his neighbor, this time he had gone to the extreme of disobedience by not going to the forced labor to which he was subjected.

The reason was to assist a young man who, since early hours, had appeared as a ghost in the enclosure where the Benefactor of the Andes resided. Using a thousand tricks, hiding from the guards and risking his own life, that soul in pain did the impossible to request Chacta's services. To tell the truth, his family was going through critical times. For some time an incurable disease had been stalking them, a kind of plague transmitted through the water they consumed. If no one prevented it, it would attack more than a hundred families.

After finding the source of the problem, Chacta gathered a good number of families and advised them very seriously to go to the quarries where clean, clear water flowed between rocks and boulders.

Chacta was a soul from another world, it was enough that a demand was formulated to him and without asking for further explanation he would nod his head and come instantly. In those moments when his presence was required, he would forget the rules and dangers and would only follow the dictates of his heart. Using recipes stored in her mind, Chacta prepared the most appropriate ointments to soothe pains and headaches that afflicted her so much. He also provided compresses and care to alleviate the sorrows of needy families.

Many hours had passed when the guards noticed his absence. Irritated, they searched for him throughout the kingdom. These facts aroused the curiosity of the anaconda who, leaving his quarters, advanced towards the construction sites, where the prisoners were working, in order to gather more information.

Chacta, the Benefactor of the Andes, was missing. That was the message that was transmitted to him. Alert! That event was the subject of a thousand reflections on the part of the anaconda, who, imagining the worst, spoke of escape. The beast, full of anger, lashed out against the helpless population.

-Bring that rebel! -the anaconda shouted indignantly.

The search intensified. Patrols of guards moved through the surroundings of the kingdom, searching every precinct, every building, every street and every labyrinth of the anaconda's domain. After an imposing raid, the guards finally found the whereabouts of Chacta, who, besieged, did not resist in order to avoid unnecessary punishment to the defenseless families.

Upon being taken to the anaconda's quarters, Chacta was severely beaten for breaking the law prohibiting all types of meetings during working hours.

However, at that moment strong vibrations of happiness shook the kingdom, affecting the mood of the anaconda. If before Chacta resented in silence, recalling past times when his heart was torn after the destruction of the Andes, now that disillusionment was leaving him. He lived moments of exaltation. For the first time he recovered his enthusiasm after so many centuries secluded in the Kingdom of Darkness.

A magical sound, like an enchanting echo, spread through the gloomy atmosphere of the numerous labyrinths, caves and nooks and crannies that formed that place, a sound that advanced, captivating thousands of lost souls with an overwhelming message, launched in a secret language that only Chacta could decipher. Secrets of past centuries that had not been revealed were finally knocking at the door.

"No more doubts," said Chacta with certainty, "the prophecy is already underway in the Andes."

Blinded by a mad enthusiasm that screamed at him that everything was possible, Chacta believed he was invincible. While the anaconda, unbalanced, swung its tail incessantly. "The moment is ripe to unleash disorder in the Kingdom of Darkness," Chacta repeated to himself, full of conviction. But the cries of the birds of the kingdom warned him to be cautious.

At that moment, a group of men, shovel in hand, approached the anaconda's quarters waiting for Chacta, who had been taken there by force. The beast was breathing heavily, spinning around as if dizzy in that foul environment. There was no better time to escape. And, without a second thought, Chacta left the beast's quarters without being discovered.

The Kingdom of Darkness was surrounded and guarded by winged animals in the service of the anaconda. Nothing escaped their penetrating gazes, and any suspicious movement was immediately transmitted to the beast through terrifying screams. The guard also had men of frightening appearance and hard faces, armed to the teeth with long chains that they used as whips to impose order.

Chacta convinced the waiting men to join his cause. During the twilight, he crossed immense swamps bounded by rocks of all sizes, in the middle of which stood the great palace of the beast. He surrounded it without encountering any of the guards. There he discreetly gathered the strongest and bravest, to whom he spoke in these terms:

"Here we are deprived of our freedom and you know well that life is something else. It is to move freely, to breathe freely, to take in the subtle smells of nature with a breath; it is not to live with a dull heart in a world plagued by misery, subjected to barbaric, cruel and violent acts where all good will vanishes into the void. This rebellion is inexorable! It is in each one of us and goes beyond our consciences! It is an outburst, an awakening, a light that urges us to say 'enough!' Yes, enough of accepting so much mistreatment."

The words of the Benefactor of the Andes penetrated into the depths of each one of those gathered there, and driven by the desire for freedom, they obeyed every order coming from Chacta. Chacta had achieved his objective and, using the discontent of those people, he proceeded to act without delay. From that moment on, the cards moved quickly: contempt and revolts broke out in the gloomy Kingdom of Darkness. The second rebellion in its history. Chacta surrounded himself with a handful of men wasted by abuse and defied rule and authority.

To the surprise of the guards, the uprising became a reality.

Chacta raised her voice to resonate within the walls of those gloomy subway caverns. A voice that traversed corridors and labyrinths until it drifted through the narrow streets and nooks and crannies. A cry that crackled in the ears of the men subjected to the abuse of the beast. Chacta told them that the time had come to rebel, that they could no longer accept this cruel domination. And thousands of slaves accepted the message of the Benefactor of the Andes.

At his signal, they marched down the corridors.

Interrupted by the bustle unfolding in the heart of her kingdom, the anaconda sat up from her throne with a blank stare and shuffled around the throne room making assumptions and trying to figure out what was going on.

Their surprised guards did not know how to react to this peculiar movement that overwhelmed them. The chiefs ran to warn the anaconda, which was seized by an indescribable rage.

"Slaves, oppressed and unarmed, break the law in my kingdom! I will deal with them myself!"

Circumstances were critical and at the construction sites the situation worsened: the rebels attacked without hesitation armed with spikes, sticks and stones. The insurgents fought with the ardor of one who fights for a just cause, with the ardor of one who stakes his life, everything for everything, until the armies of the anaconda were gradually subdued. The prospect of an uncontrollable revolt in her kingdom filled the perfidious beast with rage. And the evil ruler acted to regain control.

He mobilized his best troops, with whom he launched an operation that showed no mercy. With his intervention, the brawl took a new turn, for despite the impetus and desire to triumph, the rebels were outnumbered and were soon besieged by the guards. They lashed the insurgents with chains while monstrous birds harassed them from the air.

Chacta, in the front line to harangue the rebels, saw how the regiments of the anaconda delivered the coup de grace to the spirit of the uprising. The beast itself seized Chacta with its tail, thus capturing the indomitable instigator of that daring insurrection.

The battle ended with an overwhelming victory for the monster's armies, but the uprising had transformed the Kingdom of Darkness.

"The punishment, to be exemplary, has to be public," declared the beast.

The anger of the beast unleashed disastrous reprisals among the oppressed. After capturing the instigators, he announced that their bodies would be butchered in full view of all. So the subjects of the anaconda were forcibly rounded up and witnessed the most horrendous punishments.

In order to stand out in the dark, the beast appeared with a dazzling cloak and a mask that hid his face.

"Let it be very clear that in the Kingdom of Darkness, and also on earth, I, the anaconda, exercise absolute power. I will not allow anyone to dare to challenge my authority. These rebels will pay for the affront committed with their lives, and if you try to emulate them..., you must abide by the consequences."

And the rebels confessed that the motives that had driven them to revolt were simple: the inhabitants of that perverse world were condemned to perform forced labor for all eternity at a cadence that only a beast would be able to endure. The anaconda craved colossal renovation projects and the extension of its kingdom, and to achieve its purpose it needed manpower. The workdays were hellish, and children, women and old people fainted before such an ordeal.

Among the insurgents only one man was excluded from death: Chacta, the Benefactor of the Andes. He was brought before the anaconda under the accusation of being the mastermind of the conspiracy. Infused with rage, the beast saw in that man its bitter enemy. But it felt impotent before the impossibility of ending his life. Chacta was necessary to him.

"The day will come when you will place yourself at my service, and together we will fight for good. Even if you conspire against me, I am certain that your powers will be inoperative in the dark. You will not be able to defeat me, I can assure you of that," laughed the anaconda. For the time being you will remain my prisoner.

"Time is on my side. There is nothing you can do to stop it."

"You are wrong, Chacta. If I keep you locked in your new subway cell, I will be able to immobilize time."

"Ah, presumptuous creature! No one can stand in the way of time, nor can anyone enclose my substance. Immobility is only another form of time. The day will come when I will take a new form, and rest assured, perfidious anaconda, that from then on you will be unable to face me. Your days are numbered."

Indignant, she ordered her guards to lock Chacta in her cell. The spectacle was over, and the anaconda ordered the crowd to withdraw. Entire families marched silently away from the atrocious sight, but with the certainty that everyone's days were numbered. No plans could be made, no happiness could even be achieved. A single act of rebellion had plunged the people into barbarism. Sentenced to a life of torture, the inhabitants meekly returned to their cells with their hopes dashed.

Chacta was confined for the rest of his existence in one of the worst holes in the Kingdom of Darkness, where time faded into the damp and mud. Curiously, a strange smile lingered on his lips.

The failure of that rebellion concealed a satisfaction full of hope.

Unprotected Dolls

A few kilometers from Cuchimilcos, more precisely in the huaca of Pacha Rurac, a discussion among the members of the community of good spirits comes to an end. After hours of deliberation, Aucari concludes that, despite all efforts, they have failed to provide for the inhabitants of Cuchimilcos.

"Helébora's wrists are unprotected," she announced sadly to her family. And, if it weren't for Ollantay and Kero, she would already be disqualified. There is nothing we can do. It is the end of the adventure.

The spirits watch in disbelief. They knew that the dolls presented in the selection were simple rag dolls, but from that to wanting to abandon this beautiful project?

"How sad," they whisper to each other with broken hearts.

Obedient, they prepare for eternal sleep. In despair, Ollantay, who does not share his curaca's opinion, shakes his head disapprovingly. The word "abandonment" is not in his vocabulary. Despite his infamous reputation, he is ready to convince his people. The moment is not propitious, but using his courage he flies over them and lands in front of their leader. Inadvertently, he crushes the foot of another spirit.

Although he doesn't expect much, he takes the floor:

"We can't back out. Not now that we are so close to achieving our goals."

"It's no use rowing against the current, Ollantay," replies Aucari, discouraged and not in the mood to get angry with this energetic man. "It's over."

Ollantay's words have no effect, and Aucari gives the last instructions to leave this world. But Ollantay is stubborn and speaks of reward, of victory, of continuing the fight.

Aucari looks at him coldly and, indifferent to his speech, gives the final directives:

"We did what we could. We can't go back now, let's go!"

"The real danger is to do nothing. I refuse to believe it's all over."

Ollantay is unsettling. Aucari is sick of listening to him because he almost always talks out of his mouth and his disobedience is irritating.

"We already did the impossible when we made the protections with Helébora's help. And look at the results: those dolls wouldn't even protect a fly," Aucari concludes with an authoritative tone.

But Ollantay is stubborn.

"Helébora, despite being terrified, is still determined to show up at the fair with those rag dolls. We cannot abandon her. Her determination is an example for all of us."

Aucari observes Ollantay, for the troublemaker is right. The successive vicissitudes, sorrows and sadness have not dented the young girl's tenacity. In the face of adversity, Helébora has not given up, while he, the most resourceful, strong and courageous leader of the community of spirits, calls for her retirement. Aucari's will is broken and, with shame, she admits her fear.

"I have to confess that after seeing the lack of power of the dolls, I could not accept another failure. In the past I have not been worthy of you, I could not protect you... I am afraid that the same story is going to repeat itself..."

"We understand that," says Ollantay, "but it's not the same context. We are spirits now."

Aucari turns to Ollantay.

"You, who talk without ever keeping quiet, do you have any suggestions?"

"Well, I will go and visit the Patriarch. He possesses knowledge and will surely guide us through these difficult times."

The curaca is reluctant.

"Under these circumstances, do you still ask for advice from that man in chains?"

Although all seems lost, Aucari, lacking ideas, accepts Ollantay's proposal.

"I allow you to go to your Patriarch and ask his advice, but you will not have the right to error," he warns.

Ollantay claims to have full confidence in the Patriarch, whose advice has always been judicious. Without wasting any more time, the troublemaker sets out for the sacred mountain of Hanan Pupu.

Once there, he presents himself to the Patriarch, to whom he explains the dramatic situation in which the spirits of Pacha Rurac find themselves.

The wise man ponders for a moment before answering:

"There is no mystery about how to free Cuchimilcos from the anaconda's control: gather the original dolls that are now with the Oracle, and then bring them down to earth."

"What? Did I understand correctly? Are our dolls confined in the Oracle's temple?"

"That's right."

"And how did they get there?"

"Remember the giant bird with the twisted beak that attacked Pacha Rurac? During his retreat with the battalion of black butterflies he moved the dolls to the Oracle. I heard from the mouth of the anaconda, for his preservations resound in the Hanan Pupu, that he hid them in his sacred temple. I will give you a piece of advice to recover them: you have to tie them one by one. But not just any old way, you must use the alpaca wool ball with gold strands. Ask your textile master, he will know what I am talking about."

Back in the huaca, the anguished spirits listen to Ollantay's explanations regarding the Patriarch's advice. They need an excuse to get back to work. But, after evaluating Ollantay's words, Aucari questions his proposal:

"Too good to be true. Let's ask the textile master about this matter. He will confirm it for us."

The master of textiles, greedy for confidences, reminisces among his dramatic memories. He is dismayed at having kept such relevant information secret and confirms the veracity of the facts. The consternation is total.

"Why didn't we start with that?" many ask themselves.

"To recall the past is very painful..." replies the distressed textile master. "Yes, very painful."

"It doesn't matter what has been forgotten until today," Aucari interjected with determination. One way or another, we now have a solution. To your posts! -he orders before turning to the textile master. Our duty is to bring you the famous alpaca wool ball with gold threads, but you must know that we put our trust in you. You are the only one who can bring hope back to this land."

Unfortunately, the textile master does not know where the ball of wool has been confined. However, seeing the extreme turmoil in the community, he has no choice but to accept the challenge to try to make amends for his mistake.

"It's all right! It's all right! I'll do my best to get out of this *impasse*."

Determined to organize an expedition, Aucari mobilizes the spirit community to finalize preparations to leave the huaca. They will spare no effort.

"The time to leave has come! Hurry up! We'll divide the groups by the four of you.[9] That ball of wool has to be somewhere."

The lively, light-hearted community spreads through the air, imbued with energy. The territory is vast and the discouragement immense, especially since for centuries the community has remained cloistered in the huaca, and the geography of this remote Andean world has been transformed. However, they know well that acquiring the alpaca wool ball with gold strands is their only hope. No more excuses.

Ollantay sets off with the group in search of the ball. He emits an energy superior to the others, soaring and descending the skies. Very soon he encounters obstacles of all kinds: cold hurricane winds, narrow and inhospitable paths, deep precipices, volcanoes on the verge of exploding... After several hours of fruitless and difficult research, fatigue and discouragement take their toll on the brave spirits.

"In such a vast territory... Impossible to find something so minute. It is absurd, our efforts will lead us to nothing."

Taking into account the territory that remains to be explored, the curaca, disheartened, chooses to order the imminent return to the huaca. In spite of the countless setbacks, Ollantay does not give up and ignores the group's complaints and gripes.

"Oh no! This retreat could cost us our return to the Andes," Ollantay mutters, convinced that he is close to his goal. "Whatever happens, I will not give up."

Before night falls, Ollantay continues his search. He methodically explores every valley, grove, hill, mountain and cliff.

---

[9] 'Cardinal points' in Quechua.

Ahead he crosses a turquoise river from where a group of majestic condors take flight. It is an enchanting panorama, and Ollantay is ecstatic to breathe the pure air of the Andes. Unfortunately, he cannot stop to contemplate it. As he approaches the riverbed, he discovers a marvelous suspension bridge, a legacy from his ancestors, still standing. Ollantay recognizes the structure as part of the ancient trade route used by llama herders in times past. He examines the area for a while, the passers-by who walk through it and, in the heart of the mountains, the secret of the Incas is revealed to him. It is located next to the prestigious Sanctuary of llamas.

"Why didn't I think of that before?" -he exclaims proudly. "This is, without a doubt, the ideal place to hide the famous ball of wool."

Surrounded by green areas, sheltered by many mountains and under a bright blue sky, thousands of llamas and their cousins, the alpacas, roam freely across the vast plain. Further ahead, animals of various species stir the muddy waters of a small terrain teeming with life.

"How curious... A swamp at this altitude..."

The only vegetation is located in the swamp itself, in the form of small islands where flowers of all kinds take root. Hundreds of frogs live in the thick water, jumping in all directions. Intrigued, Ollantay observes the smallest details and writes them down in his mind, then remains for a while in that unusual place. As he moves on, the swamp becomes more animated: huge dragonflies rise above each green island, as well as other insects of all species.

Ollantay advances from discovery to discovery.

He spends a long time in this state of contemplation, absorbed by the presence of those beings that inhabit the place. At that moment, a general gathering is announced and animals flock from everywhere to a space that ends up filled with a large number of living beings. Something important is brewing.

Trying to take advantage of the situation, Ollantay penetrates a citadel whose army is mobilized to defend its queen, a *Nymphaea nelumbo* that makes a splendorous appearance in the water. "What a strange thing!" thinks Ollantay. In a full state of bloom, the *Nymphaea nelumbo* rises to the surface, where it opens up and leaves the ball of alpaca wool with gold strands for all to see.

Ollantay is astonished, he has not made a mistake! He has found what he longs for, the indispensable object for the success of his project.

"I will use all my wiles and tricks to strip this *Nymphaea nelumbo of the* alpaca wool ball with gold threads," Ollantay murmurs, full of conviction.

His eyes, as if drawn by a magnet, focus on the ball. It is so radiant, so brilliant that it eclipses any other beauty on earth. A great joy invades Ollantay. Firm and lasting joy that goes beyond his earthly understanding, proliferating contortions over his body that lead him to dive into the water.

It barely causes a few ripples when the *Nymphaea nelumbo* gathers its petals and locks itself in as if fleeing from some hidden danger. The coveted object disappears from sight.

Alerted to such a move, Ollantay withdraws cautiously without imagining that his troubles are about to begin. It is like a punishment, an anger imparted that spreads blindly by bad faith actions. In the blink of an eye, a cloud of poisonous insects approaches, every man for himself! "How to dodge them?" asks Ollantay. In those moments, the regiment advances with such ferocity that the spirit regrets being alone.

"Mercy!" cries Ollantay as his body melts. "Mercy, I don't have so much courage anymore."

But that's not all. Nearby, a platoon of giant spiders appears, throwing their silk threads to capture intruders, while poisonous frogs splash water in their wake. Although Ollantay is invisible, the insects sense his presence. "How to escape?" Cautiously, he decides to retreat.

The greatness of his ambitions has led him to act in such an unconscionable way in front of a crowd ready to lynch him. The insects only act to defend the life of their queen. Meditated and disturbed by the fault he has committed, Ollantay resolves to mature his actions and develop a precise plan that will allow him to recover the coveted alpaca wool ball with gold strands. Deep down, Ollantay has no intention of allowing himself to be intimidated by this army of insects. "There are worse things," he repeats to himself to build up his courage. And so it is that, flying over the swamp for a while, he finds a branch floating on the surface of the water.

He dives like a fish to catch it in order to use it as an instrument of defense. The timing is very uncertain and his intervention, somewhat foolish. The insects, having observed his gestures, converge on the *Nymphaea nelumbo* to protect it from the intruder and his stick. The water is murky and, fearing to be seen, Ollantay forms some whirlpools with his piece of wood to beat his way through the insects until he reaches the *Nymphaea nelumbo*. No one can resist such punishment and the insects flee.

Once in front of the flower, Ollantay delivers a fatal blow.

The impact pulls the *Nymphaea nelumbo out* of the water. Overcome by pain, it opens up, exposing the alpaca wool ball with the gold strands. Without a second thought, the spirit seizes the treasure just before a new attack of poisonous insects and takes flight back to the huaca.

In these moments of extreme feverishness, the community of spirits discusses the failure of the operation. Strutting about his achievement, Ollantay bursts into the middle of the assembly to announce the happy outcome.

"We are saved!"

And he shows before everyone the ball of alpaca wool with golden threads. The ball shines, marvels and captivates. As for Ollantay himself, he is unable to explain how he has obtained this treasure, the only thing he knows is that his act of bravery has brought back hope.

There is an explosion of joy, a new awakening.

"From now on there will be no impossibilities!" the spirits repeat to each other.

Where everything was gray, there is now light at the end of the tunnel. All that remains is to wait for the great master of textiles to do his job.

Hatun Apu

Far from all the dense agitation that surrounds the Picha Fair, a colorful boat emerges from the depths of the sea. The passengers celebrate the fact that they are about to reach their destination. On board, a flamboyant and original character jumps with joy, running at full speed through the various compartments and rooms of the ship to the first level, where he stands with longing eyes and breathes the sea breeze. At last he caresses his dream.

"Listen, we will soon arrive at the port of Callao. And there they will know who I am."

The crew nods. They are anxious to get rid of that bizarre and presumptuous individual who has caused so much trouble during the voyage. Since his embarkation, this man has caused thousands of disturbances.

It all started with a light breeze that shook him from head to toe. Asking to be attended to, the strange individual was monopolizing almost the entire staff, claiming to be suffering from sea sickness. Confronted with his multiple demands, the employees ended up detesting him. The man spent the entire voyage inventing ailments, ailments and countless complaints. And at times when he was not expressing any other discontent, he would appear unauthorized at the captain's side. And with a thick, off-key voice he would start singing.

Port, starboard. Give it your best shot, Captain.
To port, to starboard. To Peru, with the songs of sirens.

Filled with astonishment at such a fit of madness, the staff laughed out loud. But after several rehearsals they found his actions disrespectful and unfunny. The ship was full of passengers: businessmen, famous, rich and talented people who from day one had put up with this eccentric individual.

After a long voyage, the much-talked-about cruise ship arrives from Europe and as it approaches the port of Callao, a crowd of onlookers crowds to greet it. After a laborious operation of pilotage, the moorings are adjusted, the gangway is extended and the captain steps on, concluding the voyage. The passengers prepare to disembark when that unwanted individual elbows and shoves his way in.

"Let me through!" shouts the impertinent one, "Let me through!

"Sir! What are you doing?" says a passenger who is clearly holding back so as not to hit you. "Wait your turn. We are all in the same situation."

The employees, seeing the insolence of the individual, run to the gangway to avoid a brawl. And a possible scandal. Faced with such expletives, the employees gave in to the man's demands.

"All right. You will be the first to leave. Come on, get down quickly."

"I will not move from here until my server comes down with me."

"And who is that man? -The crew members ask. What's his name?"

"Chapi is his name."

Making his way through the crowd, a slender Indian of small stature and a little giddy advances carrying five jute sacks full of objects.

"But who is this man to whom so much attention is being paid? asks a tall, well-built man."

"You may not believe it, but this man is even more respected than the President of the Republic of Peru."

Upright with a haughty and slightly disgruntled air, the man disembarks followed by his faithful servant Chapi. The two remain in the port's waiting room for more than an hour.

"What the hell is going on here?" exclaims the mysterious man. "I need my bags, how slow!"

"Relax, sir," the longshoremen reply. "We do what we can."

"One thing is for sure: I will not come to Peru anymore."

"I don't want to antagonize you, but if you don't want to wait here, you can come back tomorrow to claim your belongings."

"Tomorrow, tomorrow... That is the favorite word of the idle."

Trapped in this nightmare, his first impulse is to demand to be attended to. With eyes full of rage, a reddened face and an expression of insolence, the man rushes forward to demand an explanation for the delay, while Chapi tries to calm him down to prevent him from committing another nonsense.

"I want to speak to the director," requests the man with an altered tone.

"The director is currently in a meeting."

"For God's sake, do something! I can't wait any longer."

"We do what we can. Unfortunately, the arrival coincides with the Picha Fair and at this time of the year there is a lot of demand."

Despite the incessant complaints, the port employees are not surprised, as they are used to dealing with such customers.

Amidst the hustle and bustle, the cruise ship's luggage finally arrives.

"Please step aside," exclaim the employees carrying the packages."

"I need my luggage!" shouts the man out of control.

Suitcases fall here and there with a clatter, rolling on the smooth floor of the port. Disgruntled, the man rummages through the luggage, touching one and another, throwing them everywhere. Many are displeased with such an act and the police have to intervene in the commotion, beating back the disgruntled people with sticks.

"What's going on here?"

"It's that man!" the passengers exclaim. "That disrespectful man is getting on our nerves."

"Whoever dares to hit this man will go to jail, because he is a living legend and Peru needs him."

The passengers calm down in the face of the threats, but the man continues with his circus while his assistant searches for the most appropriate way to transport the belongings. After several hours, the number of suitcases dwindles and the frustrated man remains at the port waiting for his most precious treasure.

"I can't believe it, this is all a joke! Yes, a ridiculous mockery to make me lose my patience."

"Please do not despair. You will get the rest of your luggage back very soon."

"Don't you understand that I can't wait any longer? I have to leave this damned port right now."

Suddenly, the loudspeakers announce an important message.

"A technical problem prevents us from continuing with the unloading of luggage. A suitcase of exceptional size and shape is stuck."

"It's probably my box," says the man.

"Describe it," asks one of the dock workers.

"It has the appearance of a sarcophagus."

"Yes, that's right. Sir, please come with me."

To the bewilderment of the onlookers, the mysterious man and his assistant wander through the corridors of the port, getting lost in the crowd. At the end of the path awaits his unmistakable suitcase, stiff as a dead man. The man moves forward smiling, deftly dodging the objects that roll on the floor. He points to the sarcophagus and a young porter approaches him with an air of guilt.

"Your box has suffered a slight crack."

"Impossible! It's made to last forever. Don't worry, my boy, nothing has happened to it. You'll see how a thorough inspection will convince you that it was only an illusion."

The loader turns to ask for help, as he needs to unload the precious cargo. Supervised by the owner of the crate, five underfed youngsters are suffocating under its weight.

"What can this damned sarcophagus contain?"

"Wait a minute," interrupts the man, "I'm not going to allow you to express yourselves that way. It's art you're talking about. Hurry up and be careful because at the slightest fall you will be cursed for the rest of your days.

With sudden movements, the boys deposit the heavy cargo in front of the man, who impatiently approaches with his assistant.

"Let's go. Check that everything is all right."

Chapi, with his legendary dexterity, moves and removes the sarcophagus, examining every angle, but unknown voices interrupt the process. They are port employees.

"And what do they want now?" exclaims the mysterious man in disbelief.

"What's in that box? -Are these real mummies?"

"No, I simply use an ancient technique to protect my most valuable objects."

"What a strange way to prepare for a trip. Do you have anything to declare, sir?"

"No! Everything I am carrying belongs to me. I have nothing to declare, and now let me pass."

"Listen, you must at least tell us what you keep in that colossal sarcophagus."

"Working tools," replies the owner. "It's about art, just art."

"All right," say the workers, unconvinced. "Follow me, please."

"Look, young man, it's been more than three hours that I've been waiting in this infectious port. There is a limit to my patience. I have with me a form which I was made to fill out and of which you should keep a copy. Now, let me go."

After a few checks, the man finally leaves the port. Exhausted and fatigued by so much delay, he just wants to rest. He orders his servant to take care of his belongings while he leaves in search of a transport to take him to his destination.

Chapi throws a rope over the huge cargo and packs the sarcophagus, the sacks of jute and the suitcases with a single knot, dragging them slowly to prevent them from falling. He catches up with his master amidst the admiring glances of the curious onlookers in the harbor. After the precious cargo is placed on the transport that his master has obtained, they are taken to the Bolivar Hotel, where the owner throws a juicy sum that allows him to enter the interior without saying a word.

There, away from the hustle and bustle associated with his arrival, the man stops at the doors of the hotel, where he turns to his assistant.

"Lay down the red carpet, I have to get through!" Chapi hurries to comply with the order. "You're very lucky you weren't born in ancient times," he says as he watches his eager assistant. Otherwise, you would have welcomed me with flower petals and giant feathers to air out the passageway, thus preventing the sun from touching me.

"What era are you talking about, boss?"

"Are you Peruvian or are you not?"

"Yes, but..."

"You have to educate yourself, you idiot! I'm wasting my time with you. How stupid! You ignore the most important thing: the treatment reserved for great and glorious personalities."

The hotel employees, after witnessing all the pomp of the entrance, go out to find out what is going on.

"Who is this individual?"

But the man, who has a keen ear, answers them by advancing on the red carpet:

"I am the undisputed master of goldsmithing. I need two rooms, the more modest one for my assistant and the more luxurious one for me. I want my room to have tapestry, works of art and flowers, for I need to be surrounded by beauty. Oh, I forgot! Do you have a room with hot springs? "

"No, sir. But we can offer you a room with sauna."

"Sauna? It doesn't suit me."

"The rooms are very comfortable and luxurious. You can visit them."

"Well..., anyway, I won't stay long. I want my meals in my room. I don't want to eat with anyone. Send me the menu three times a day so I can choose."

"Well, sir."

"Another point. I need a balcony to breathe and go out to admire the beautiful city of Lima. I have just come from a long trip and I am very tired. I would also like to request the services of a professional masseuse. Oh, I forgot! And a complete treatment for my aching feet. One last request: I don't want to be disturbed. I will open the door only to the services requested. Is that clear?"

"Yes, sir. Don't worry. We are at your service. Here are your keys. We'll take care of your luggage and call the best masseuse in town."

The hotel is the most prestigious in the capital of Peru. But for the man nothing is inaccessible. Life has been a feather in his cap since his birth. His good star accompanies him wherever he is through the years. This man is the whim of many rich and famous women, for he represents glory, fame, prestige and also vanity.

The days go by and the man recovers his strength among massages, sumptuous food and good treatment. He leaves behind all those embarrassing moments of his arrival on Peruvian soil. Finally the day of his departure arrives and he does not miss the opportunity to announce his departure with great fanfare.

"What kind of fuss is that? -the employees ask themselves."

"I need the best car in town," declares the guest. The most luxurious and fancy, because that's what I deserve."

"Your wishes will be fulfilled."

After a quarter of an hour, a limousine pulls up at the entrance of the Bolivar hotel.

"Good morning," says the chauffeur, "with whom do I have the pleasure?"

"I cannot confess my name. However, I stir the happiest and saddest memories in the heart of every Peruvian. I am a song, a living tradition, a poem, a rhyme. He who knows me reveres me and desires me. I am the sunrise and the sunset, the sun and the moon, the serenity and the storm. I am a living legend..."

"Where do you want to go, sir?" asks the chauffeur, trying to contain his laughter.

"Take me to the bus station."

Half an hour later, the man and his servant arrive at their destination. The bus depot has become an anthill of activity.

Everything is bustling as overheated passengers fight for a seat and others patiently wait their turn seated in the seats.

"Where can I rent a bus for me and my assistant?" he asks for information. "I have to go to Picha."

"A bus for two passengers? You have lost all sanity. Get in line, sir. I think the waiting is driving you crazy."

"You misunderstood me. Listen to me: I want to rent a bus for me and my assistant. And I insist that I have no time to lose. Get up and look for your employer."

The employee, seeing the customer's determination, leaves the information booth and runs in search of the store manager.

"Mr. Gutierrez, there is an individual outside who wants to rent a bus for himself and his assistant."

"For what purpose?"

"Picha."

"That man is sick. I have no intention of losing sixty passengers, plus those we pick up along the way, just to satisfy the whims of a poor idiot. Go and throw him out of here. Or, better yet, tell him to stand in line like any other passenger."

"I already told him, but he still insists."

"What? Take care of him, I don't want to know anything."

"Okay."

Back at the booth, the employee shakes his head as he addresses the traveler.

"Impossible, sir! Get out of here. Don't waste any more of our time. We're overworked and understaffed. Please leave."

In the face of the refusal, the mysterious man, true to himself, offers a forceful monetary settlement.

"Listen to me. I'm willing to pay five times what a full bus will get you. I don't have much time and I need to leave right now."

With the last sentence, he deposits such an impressive wad of bills on the table that the employee leaves again to consult with his employer. This time Mr. Gutierrez himself wants to meet the mysterious man. The negotiation concludes between bargaining and offering. And that is how the stranger departs accompanied by his assistant before the astonished looks of the people waiting at the bus station.

"We wish you a good trip," says Mr. Gutiérrez.

"Thank you."

There is a fleet of buses heading in the same direction. The man and his assistant are on one of the vehicles, vanishing into the endless roads that lead to the Peruvian highlands. The exhalations of dust and black smoke excite the man and as his heart beats with uncontainable force he watches them drive away from the station.

"What a joy! I will soon be in Picha."

The landscapes are the same. The passing years have not changed them. Overcome by a terrible nostalgia, his eyes do not resist shedding a few tears. The man observes the marvelous change from day to night, and later admires the starry sky over the mountains.

"I ask you, little star that enlightens me, that this visit be the most beautiful that my heart will ever remember."

Under the darkness of the arid and abandoned road, the bus crosses the last villages on the way to Picha. At the end of the journey, the summit of your dream city is announced.

"It's Picha I can make out! -shouts the excited man."

"Yes, sir," says the driver, "We are approaching the outskirts of the city of Picha."

The bus stops at the main square of the city.

"I need to go to the El Jilguero hotel," the man says to the driver. "Please continue. Don't leave us in the plaza."

When he gets off the bus, the owner of the establishment immediately recognizes him.

"What a joy, what a pleasant surprise! From today this land is blessed."

The mysterious man embraces him with a smile.

"It has been a long time, Don Anselmo, but over the years we always retrace the same steps."

"Yes, that's true," agrees Don Anselmo, "I have left the hustle and bustle of the capital to settle here, in my homeland. The hotel is fully booked, are you coming to live in Picha?"

"No! For the moment I'm only coming to the fair. Maybe later I will stay for the rest of my days."

"But don't worry, I'll find you accommodation in no time. I'll be evicting two clients. You will have the main room and your assistant will sleep in a simpler room, as usual."

"This trip has exhausted me. Tell me, don Anselmo, may I bathe in the hot springs?"

"Let me take a look. I will notify my clients to evict them."

"I would like to ask you a favor: don't tell anyone that I'm here. Oh, I forgot! Do you have a calendar of the fair's activities?"

"Of course. Here you go and don't worry, your visit will be kept in the deepest secrecy."

After a relaxing and restorative bath, the man sleeps for eight hours straight in his room. Two weeks later, the opening of the Picha Fair is announced, and locals and visitors crowd in front of the wrought iron gates.

The official day awaits them.

For his part, the man prepares with his assistant to go to the fair. Juancho Hatun Apu, that is his name. Recently arrived in the Andes after a long self-imposed exile, he finally returns to his land, to his people. And his heart beats strongly in the moments before he reveals himself to the world.

An Insistent Suitor

Helébora barely sleeps the night before the dreaded day she must take the biggest leap of her short life. With a small pang in her heart, she approaches the window to contemplate the chain of hypnotizing Andean mountains. Daylight is rising in the firmament over a clear and unimpeded sky, with a quiet cadence that seems like a maybe yes, maybe no.

"Oh, tender heavenly light! Fill me with your purity. Protect me from unknown directions and take me to solid ground where I know neither pain nor disappointment."

Sixteen years old, Helébora meditates on tomorrow as she prepares for the first day of October. The cold of her mountains announces that today will be the big day.

Leaving her dreams on Hanan Pupu, the sacred mountain, she dresses up to go to the Picha Fair. Fortunata gathers her dense, luxuriant hair in a braid that ends with red ribbons. Then the moment of departure arrives and, moving towards the dolls, Helébora takes out the jute bags she has sewn and then carefully introduces her prodigious creations. After a moment, when everything is packed, a barrage of whispers and requests invade Fortunata's living space.

"We need the Inca vessels. You have to bring them."

"Who is this? -asks the mother."

A fleeting rush of cold air causes the glasses to rattle, making little buzzing noises. Putting aside her surprise, Fortunata pulls and secures them with two thick slats to take them out of the house and place them on the backs of two llamas.

"Mom, what are you doing with those glasses?"

"A voice told me we will need these Inca vessels for this great day. Prepare also the llamas and the carts, decorate them coquettishly while I wash my hair."

Clinging to a tree branch that serves him as a cane, Don Gumersindo climbs with great difficulty the steep slope that leads him to Helébora's house. The door is closed, but when he opens it, the girl from the mountains appears resplendent.

"Are you ready?"

"Don Gumersindo, what a surprise! Yes, God willing."

"Don't worry, Helébora, since you are sheltered by the mountains."

"May God hear you, Don Gumersindo. May God hear you."

The carts are finally ready with the dolls inside. Helébora counts them while Don Gumersindo lavishes her with warm and encouraging words. The young woman is satisfied and they set off. The wise man accompanies the women on their descent down the steep road and helps them pull the wagons. And amidst darkness and fog, Helébora, her mother and don Gumersindo descend. The stops are constant, as the two wagons are loaded and force them to stop to catch their breath.

"Be careful, my daughter. Watch your step. We can't allow any doll to fall, otherwise we'll be cursed for the rest of our days.

The village healer approaches them, emanating a smell of incense.

"We are proud of you. I have come to help you."

Helébora is pleased and gives way to the new loader. When they finally descend the slope, they find a gigantic crowd in the central square. When they get there, Helébora, her mother and don Gumersindo are speechless. The entire town of Cuchimilcos gives its all to support her on this special day. It is moving to see so many men, women and children sharing this joy.

"Long live our Helébora, the protégée of the Andes!"

The sound of the quenas, the pututos and even the harp of don Gumersindo. And, pushing the wagons, a group of men advance while Helébora and her mother guide the llamas. The whole village follows them. After hours of walking, they catch sight of the town of Picha.

"We're near the fair, Mom."

Nervous and unable to contain herself, Helébora takes one of the dolls and squeezes it tightly against her chest and then scrutinizes the smallest details with her fingers. She asks if her work will be up to the event.

"We have never seen such real dolls," the people reply.

Leaving the foothills of the mountains behind, Helébora succumbs to the nostalgic melodies of the Andes. The groups entertain the attendees at the Picha Fair with their magical songs.

> Where are you going, palomitay?
> so hurried and light, palomitay,
> be careful in the wind, palomitay,
> I send you my breath, palomitay.

Helébora, with tears in her eyes, says goodbye to her beloved town and its inhabitants. A colorful and joyful city opens before her. The smells of incense and eucalyptus impregnate the air with aromas that combine with those of various dishes. Crowded in the streets of Picha, a crowd prepares for the opening of the fair.

Helébora is pleased to feel surrounded by all that enthusiasm after many months of confinement and receives it as the most precious gift that life can offer her. She arrives fascinated at the main gate of the fair.

"Are you a craftswoman?" asks the doorman.

"Yes, sir."

"Go ahead, welcome to the establishment of creation. And this woman?"

"It's my mother, she comes with her llamas to keep me company."

"It's all right. You come in too, ma'am."

Helébora is very nervous. She scans the surroundings to grasp at something familiar. Her expressive eyes silently watch the faces of familiar artisans. Helébora notices that the grounds are covered with vases of fresh flowers. In some corners musicians repeat over and over again the bars and melodies they are going to present, while folkloric groups rehearse dances on the stands. Small theaters are set up in different places. Incense and smoke permeate the atmosphere. The organizers pronounce a prayer and invite the exponents to join in the prayer. Holding hands, they give thanks to the Lord.

A line forms to place each artisan in his assigned kiosk. A line that advances at a snail's pace in the sweltering heat. Everyone questions whether it makes sense to remain in the sun. The director explains, making himself heard over the noise of the place, that at the close of the fair a reward will be given to the most sought-after artist: the golden pelican.

He raises it and the director emphasizes that this symbol, the product of a long-standing tradition, will be the most precious object that an artisan can keep in his workshop.

But on that particularly hot morning, the fair welcomes a mysterious visitor. Exhibitors lined up waiting to be seated when a man of overwhelming fame made his appearance. The organizers are fascinated and come to pay their respects.

"God has made the miracle! Don Juancho Hatun Apu, what brings you to these modest lands?"

"I have come from far away to exhibit my latest creations."

"Our fair has not received such an illustrious craftsman for many years. Come in, you are welcome."

Helébora is standing in line when Don Juancho Hatun Apu gives her a slight push to move her, as she is going to be the next to be assigned to a kiosk. Noticing the touch on her arm, Helébora turns her head slightly and don Juancho realizes that in front of him is the most beautiful creature his eyes have ever seen.

The girl presses the wrist bag against her chest and bows her head to hide her nervousness. She does not know that she is in front of the master of masters, but she sees that he is showered with praise and good treatment, forgetting her completely. At that moment she does not understand the reason for so much attention and, leaning to one side, she hurriedly asks who is the man who is causing so much commotion.

> He is the most prodigious goldsmith that the world has ever engendered. Juancho Hatun Apu is his name, but he works under the nickname of "he who beautifies everything with his hands". Don Juancho is a direct descendant of the most respected goldsmith dynasty of the Inca Empire, intimately linked to the Inca nobility. It is said that the strong bond that united his family with the Inca descendants goes back to the time when the young prince Viracocha, the eighth sovereign, was expelled from the sacred city of Cusco due to his bellicose and rebellious behavior. During his exile, a member of the Hatun Apu clan joined in friendship with the prince.

Viracocha saw in him a faithful friend who did not cease to offer him objects in gold and silver as a token of friendship. Years later, due to the attacks and hostilities of the charcas, the city of Cusco was abandoned by his sovereign father, who sought refuge in the outskirts. The alarming news reached the prince's ears through a celestial apparition of the god Wiracocha himself, who entrusted him to defend the unprotected city. Thanks to his courage and bravery, the prince Viracocha subdued the invaders in a memorable battle where even the stones allied with him to defend the city of the sun. After the so resounding victory Viracocha was named the next Inca. As soon as he was installed in the sacred city of the Incas, Viracocha sent for the Hatun Apu family, who from that memorable moment became the most respected goldsmiths of the empire.

The Hatun Apu clan actively participated in the decoration of royal residences, sanctuaries and temples for the virgins of the sun. At the same time, they produced the finest garments of the empire, sewn and adorned with gold thread, which were offered to the most prestigious curacas of the time. Their work spoke for itself: numerous details, great delicacy and creativity. The only reason for the Hatun Apu family to live was to let creativity run free. The Inca never intervened in their works, because they were so expert that the Inca hardly explained what he wanted. The creative ideas circulated in the minds of the family and the works were so perfect that they always pleased the sovereign. That knowledge was transmitted from generation to generation.

At the time of the conquest, the Hatun Apu family was at the side of the last legitimate Inca Huayna Capac. At the death of Huascar, the Hatun Apu understood that nothing kept them in Cusco and decided to leave it definitively. Upon their departure the Hatun Apu learned that Atahualpa, the last Inca held captive by the mounted men, promised to gather the most important treasure that the whole world had ever gathered and offered his captors a room full of gold and two rooms full of silver. But he was executed.

Deeply displeased by that act, the Hatun Apu family decided to hide the treasures they guarded at an altitude of more than four thousand meters, where the white man would never loiter. The night that followed Atahualpa's execution, they secretly ascended the mountains accompanied by several llamas laden with treasures. The Hatun Apu kept their promises and hid the treasure in the highest peaks of the Andes, hidden among the clouds. It is said that they buried the precious cargo in the depths of a cave. When they finished, they settled in the heights of the mountains, where they would never be discovered. From then on, the Hatun Apu only descended to look for provisions that would allow the hundred or so people who made up the community living in the heights to subsist. Centuries later, they learned that the men on horseback had abandoned the Andes for good. It was then that they left the altitude to settle in the city of Cusco, where they continued to practice their profession. They are still recognized as the best goldsmiths in the country.

"You are very kind," says Helébora, "Thank you for informing me.

In an instinctive desire not to go unnoticed by that girl, Don Juancho Hatun Apu asks for more details about her as he watches the artisan walk away.

"Her name is Helébora Rumi, and this is her first year. The girl is going to exhibit the famous Chancay dolls. That is all we can tell you.

"That young lady will be my assistant, I need her. She is the most beautiful hostess that the Andean mountains can provide."

"How long will you be with us, Don Juancho?"

She receives no response to her inquiry. In the meantime, Helébora is attended to and assigned a red ribbon.

"Since you are a novice and inexperienced artisan, your kiosk will be located at the back, near the terral. Don't worry, there is plenty of land."

"What about my mother?"

"She will go with you."

Mother and daughter have barely finished settling in when Hatun Apu shows up.

"What are you doing here, sir?" Fortunata asks. "Can I help you?"

"Excuse me, I just came to wish you good luck."

"To us? And why?"

"Because this is the first time you are exhibiting at the fair."

"Yes, that's right," Helébora replied with a blush, "Thank you very much, sir."

"You can call me Juancho, my beauty. Call me Juancho."

"All right."

"Listen, bella. I don't want to appear grotesque or ridiculous, but I would like to confess something to you."

"Yes, say."

"You are the most beautiful creature my eyes have ever seen."

Embarrassed, Helébora lowers her gaze and turns around blushing. Never has a man expressed himself in such a way. Hatun Apu immediately understands that flattery does not work with that young girl. His first attempt has failed and he must be very careful. Without giving Helébora time to react, Hatun Apu decides to change tactics.

"I apologize if I offended you. I am very sorry. That was not my intention."

And feeling sorry for her, he takes her by the hand.

"Are these princess hands that have made these wonderful dolls?"

"Yes."

"If it's not too much to ask, what's your name?"

"Helébora. Helébora Rumi, sir."

"What a strange name, surely there is an enigma behind it. But how beautiful it is," says Hatun Apu. "Look, Helébora, you don't need to sell your dolls. You can close your kiosk now because I'll buy them all. I have a lot of money. Take advantage of this opportunity, because you will only get it once."

That is Hatun Apu's offer. Then he shakes his hands in the air, showing off his diamond and solid gold rings. Helébora is outraged. She can't understand how an unscrupulous man could offer her that kind of business. She, who has made so many sacrifices to attend the fair, who has worked so hard to make more than a hundred dolls...

"I have come a long way for the Andean people to get a copy," she replies irritably. "I don't sell just anything. This is about protection."

Hatun Apu hastens to apologize when he sees the aversion that his stupid reasoning arouses.

"I am very sorry. You misunderstood my words, my only intention was to secure your sales. Well, I'll take my leave. I think I've already said a lot of nonsense."

Muttering through his teeth about his blunder, Hatun Apu walks off crestfallen towards the organizers, whom he angrily accosts.

"I need the stand to exhibit my objects. I cede to another craftsman the kiosk that has been assigned to me. I also need curtains, a table, a microphone and an assistant. I want you to convince Helébora, the young woman from the last kiosk."

Like an elusive wind, the spirits that accompany the young girl murmur in her ear:

"This is your chance, don't miss it."

Strangely, Helébora walks towards Hatun Apu's kiosk with a sack of dolls. Seeing her approaching, Hatun Apu waits anxiously for her.

"Welcome, Helébora Rumi."

The spirits, ecstatic, embrace each other because of the unexpectedness of the situation, so propitious to bring a new talent out of anonymity.

With obvious relief at how everything has been resolved, the organizers continue with their busy work while the table, curtains and microphone for Hatun Apu arrive.

Helébora is decked out in a long one-piece dress and a belt that showcases her curves and her lanky, shapely body. One would say she has reached perfection. Added to that are her long jet black hairs, which fall delicately down her shoulders and lose their way down her back. She covers her feet with sandals that she has made herself. The girl fascinates by her fragility, simplicity and shyness.

However, being the assistant to the master teacher - what a challenge!

The organizers call the crowd to order while the thirsty crowd advances in flocks, squeezing against each other. Pushing and elbowing are commonplace and some of them end up falling to the ground after so much pushing and shoving, only to be crushed by countless stormy footsteps. Badly wounded, some require first aid while the rest move in various directions. And, in the face of so much confusion, a thick and imposing voice is heard through the microphones:

"The master of masters, the famous don Juancho Hatun Apu, is here. He is waiting for you on the central dais."

Like a rising tide, the audience rushes to the right place. The spirits watch in astonishment at the outcome.

"Impossible, we can't do anything," they say to each other.

Almost the entire crowd crowds in the central stage, where between curtains, whispers and vociferations the celebrity is presented to his audience.

"I am don Juancho Hatun Apu, the master of masters."

The artisan performs a spectacular number and the spectators, eager to contemplate the perfect work, remain motionless in their seats. The applause rains down on him and the audience does not cease to cry out the name of the blessed goldsmith. Suddenly, the scene opens completely and in the middle of the table a voluminous sarcophagus is revealed.

"Good morning, my beautiful audience. It is a great honor to spend a few days with you. I am very happy to see that after so many years of absence, beauty has not been lost in the Andes. It is with great pleasure and pride that I present my assistant, Miss Helébora Rumi. Please welcome her with a strong and warm applause."

And, following the goldsmith's instructions, the gallery acclaims the girl. The ovation is tremendous, as if she were a renowned artist.

"Did you know that when Hel ebora came into the world a bunch of stars appeared in the sky and then became a constellation? The sun laughed with joy; the moon danced on one foot; the vegetation was in full bloom; the sea and the mountains sang; and the valleys, animals and stones radiated with happiness."

The audience laughs at his unusual witticisms and Hatun Apu spreads his good humor. Once the hubbub dies down, the master continues:

"Today you will be perplexed by what you are about to witness. Did you know that only archaeologists and wise men have been allowed to observe what I am about to show you? A technique that has been used and passed down for generations to preserve our loved ones. I now use it in my daily life to protect my most precious objects."

Hatun Apu shows, piece by piece, while the spectators remain perplexed, without missing any detail of the master's explanation. Helébora takes beautiful textiles and steps aside to show them in her hands while waiting for the expert to pronounce himself. Hatun Apu scrutinizes every detail of the textiles, every motif, revealing the origin, who made it, who used it, how it was found and even how it was protected until it finally fell under his custody. Many are the textiles that parade before the avid eyes of this interested public.

For the end he reserves jewels from the Inca period. Hatun Apu dwells on each of these, explaining again the type of material used in their manufacture, always making a journey through history. At the request of the master, Helébora wears each jewel while he bewitches with his teachings.

Helébora must admit that Hatun Apu is an excellent speaker. His facility with the verb attracts crowds. As the days go by, the lines seem endless and don Juancho responds one by one to the requests of the public. The master is passionate about his art, his past makes him proud, and he offers forceful explanations with great confidence. However, Hatun Apu must leave the fair on a precise date, for commercial reasons. And on the eve of his departure, he informs the organizers.

His withdrawal falls like a bucket of cold water among those responsible for the event, who, unable to keep him, organize a small ceremony in homage to such a worthy goldsmith. The artisans of the fair shower him with gifts and, amidst hugs and applause, Hatun Apu prepares to leave the premises, but not before handing over his data to Helébora.

The craftsmen give way to the man who needs to know the girl's reaction before leaving. He thinks he has glimpsed in her experience of work and life, and, above all, an enigmatic personality.

"Helébora," he calls her. "Where are you?"

"Here I am, sir."

"Here you go, beautiful. Here is my address. I will always be available for you, whether it is to teach you goldsmithing techniques, to let you in on a tailoring secret, to give you advice or for any other reason. Rest assured that the doors of my heart will always be open to you. Before leaving, tell me one thing: where do you come from?"

"From Cuchimilcos," replies Helébora, smiling.

"Cuchimilcos! I don't know it. I imagine it is a remote little village in the Andes. Your life must be difficult and full of obstacles."

Helébora listens without answering. Hatun Apu takes advantage of the occasion to give her one of his best pieces, a charm with the image of Tumi.

"Keep it with you," said the master, smiling. "I offer you this simple souvenir in memory of this beautiful friendship that unites us. And I ask you, please, to keep it with you always."

Surprised by the gift, Helébora does not know what to say. The gift is very ostentatious; she has never received anything like it in her life. She hurries to her kiosk, where she picks up a doll and offers it to the goldsmith.

"My present is very modest, but I give it to you from my heart. You are a man of remarkable nobility and I will never forget your generosity, but I cannot accept this jewel."

Hatun Apu insists, begging and pleading, and Helébora finally accepts the gift. More cheerful, the master leaves the fair playing an ancient yaraví:

Caylla llapi.
Puñunqui
chaupituta,
samusac.[10]

_____
[10] 'Between songs you will sleep, at midnight I will return'.

It is the first time she has spoken Quechua since her arrival in Peru. However, Helébora does not react to such a manifestation of lyricism, but turns her head and ends her participation.

"Come back to see me for what?" she asks herself a little surprised.

For the first time in his life, Hatun Apu feels ignored and rebuffed as his advances are not welded into a meeting, an oath, a "don't go away" or any other proof of affection. Hatun Apu realizes that his efforts have been fruitless. Frustrated, his disgruntled movements reach Dantesque proportions and he prefers to opt for violent actions, shaking his head from one end to the other, moving disorderly, sometimes jumping, sometimes, advancing and retreating. He picks up the doll and goes to the young woman's kiosk.

Don Juancho Hatun Apu is furious, throwing sparks with an air of discontent as if he intended to kill her with his gaze.

"My little flower of the Andes, always remember that I will return. Memorize this: 'At noon I will arrive, at midnight I will leave and I will break your heart.'" He bids farewell to the young girl with a wave of his hand. "I will return, I will return. Be sure of that, Helébora. I will come back."

Then, his voice cracks as he moves away from the fair, as if he had cast a spell from the depths of his being. As he walks away, Hatun Apu watches Helébora out of the corner of his eye. He is the master of dissimulation and wishes that on this occasion his gestures had not betrayed him.

Hatun Apu leaves the fair due to his commercial commitments, but the truth is that he could have cancelled them if Helébora had simply asked him to do so, but with this cold and indifferent reaction the young woman has broken the goldsmith's heart. Her dry lips, cracked by so much anger, express a restrained rage and her disgruntled gestures show the inner turmoil she is going through. Deep down she imagines that Helébora will be subjugated to her charms and that she will soon be begging him, unhinged, not to leave.

But this is not the case.

Don Juancho Hatun Apu leaves Picha followed by his servant Chapi.

Helébora is shocked, the initial joyful uproar has turned into a horrible nightmare. Never before has a man cursed her with such an indignant, dark voice and such disgruntled gestures. The young girl can swear that the man is unhinged. The audience, witnessing these senseless reactions, excuses Juancho Hatun Apu's actions.

"Poor man. Love has upset him."

After this fateful incident, Helébora is convinced that from now on her destiny will be marked by those phrases that echo in her mind like a destructive echo. However, that enigmatic man has brought her luck. Her kiosk fills up with visitors without any effort and the curious are interested in the origin of the dolls, the reason for their presentation, the price and other things.

Helébora feels a new wind blowing in her favor.

The First
Ray of Happiness

Helébora has been disturbed for a long time. She has felt Hatun Apu's last words as an insult to her. Unsettled, she is unable to focus while the audience wonders if that charming face can still delight them with some stories about the Chancay dolls she exhibits. Call it curiosity or simply a penchant for occult mysteries. There are many who implore him for a story.

The interest is clear, no matter if the dolls are unprotected. The spirits accompanying Helébora understand that the dolls' memorable identity is about to be revealed. They redouble their efforts to welcome customers. They hastily move through the air and lead the flames to a vacant lot, which they examine until they are satisfied. That's what they need.

A black, rough and dirty terral that is blown away by the gales that they themselves provoke as they fly through the air. A dense dust rises in swirls and settles on the handmade samples of other kiosks. The ground, now free of dirt, is decorated with bright colors where the dolls glitter, then the spirits form a small mound on which they place a white flame. Realizing that they will need a floral environment, they bring eucalyptus branches, clay pots, copper pots, stylized and deformed, as many as they can gather.

Helébora, who is still recovering from the unpleasant experience with the goldsmith, shows the dolls to an agitated audience that insists on the telling of ancient stories involving the dolls. Surprised by the request, Helébora looks around the glittering terral and accepts the challenge. The girl walks slowly, inviting the spectators to follow her until she fills the large space.

It is eleven o'clock on a sweltering morning, and Helébora, with a wrist in each hand, rides the white flame. The girl is gleaming. Although there is no shade in which to shelter, the crowd moves excitedly towards the young girl, imagining that they will be moved by surprising stories. Helébora smiles as her mind wanders to the memories of her childhood, when as a child she gathered llamas, alpacas and some dogs to tell them a few stories, some of them made up, some of them heard from the locals. Some made up, others heard from her own mother. Believing that she was impressing her animal audience, she would touch them one by one to collect the impressions of their gestures and looks. This is the origin of Helébora's storytelling practice.

It is almost noon when the curious, huddled together like bees in a honeycomb, become insistent.

"We've been here for more than half an hour. We can't wait any longer. What time will the storyteller start?"

Helébora feels unhinged in those moments of turmoil, lost in her fears. Sitting on the flame on that radiant day, the fear of not being up to the task dominates her, along with a deep nervousness that makes her legendary bravery fade. Between requests and applause, Helébora tries to calm down, but she loses herself in an ocean of confusion.

"Why me? How did I get here?"

Faced with their unending disquiet, the spirits appointed by the curaca gather to fix the impending disaster.

"Impossible! We cannot allow it. Helébora must tell the stories of the Chancay dolls. They are many and each one more captivating. Poet spirit, help this young girl and make this experience a total success."

Seeking the protection of the invisible, Helébora implores her protective spirits to guide her. Suddenly, she hears a small, shimmering voice.

"Don't be afraid, we are with you. The stories will follow their normal course and tell themselves."

This is how Helébora regains the poise and confidence that characterizes her. The poet spirit whispers a chronicle of ancient times and the girl modulates her voice to address the audience. A narration begins, one that alludes to the hidden city of Chamac.

His people were fierce and brave, but they suffered a siege of several months, perpetrated by the charcas. Short of food and water, the people of Chamac tried to free themselves and break the circle that was suffocating them. Led by their best generals, they prepared themselves for energetic fights, attacks and counterattacks. Despite their bravery, after several days of fighting, the Chamac army succumbed to the large enemy army. The mortally wounded Chamac leader asked his messenger to announce to the citadel the inevitable victory of the charcas. The messenger collapsed exhausted in the center of the square. The inhabitants rushed to offer him help, and that is when the messenger delivered his painful missive. "The charcas! The charcas!" he shouted. As he uttered those terrifying words, the inhabitants understood the gravity of the situation. In their desperation, the villagers rushed to tear down the Mamacona bridge, access to the citadel. "They will not have time to destroy the bridge," said the half-dead messenger. They are very close to the citadel. Go and hide. Women, children and old men took refuge in the sanctuary of their god. Others, fearful, scattered into the forest. Most children owned a Chancay doll, and asking what to do with their dolls one woman suggested placing them at the entrance of the citadel. Imploring their dolls with unusual fervor, the citizens begged for their lives.

Emboldened, the leader of the charcas advanced at a victorious pace across the old and narrow bridge of the Mamacona, sure of his victory because he knew beforehand that all his enemies had succumbed in the bloody battles. He surveyed the citadel with great arrogance and with a broad smile of triumph advanced with his troop. When he crossed the Mamacona, he ordered to kill every living being and to take possession of the citadel. The army was on its way to the central square when the chief, having gone ahead, saw with curiosity the hundreds of dolls scattered on the floor of the square. Intrigued by that sight, the chief approached to get a better look at them. "But what mockery is this? Get these dolls out of my way," he ordered. But the charcas soldiers could not carry out the command, for the dolls opened their eyes as if they were alive and a gloomy twilight covered the sky with dark darkness. The dolls moved their eyes in unison, covered with tears, and a torrent of cries and complaints burst from their mouths in an unknown language. Hearing such deep groans, and seeing that the pale sun was fading away to give way to darkness, the charcas implored their god. A deluvian rain accompanied by lightning and unrestrained thunder rushed over the central square of the citadel. The charcas immediately understood that their god was in a rage and retreated without a second thought.

It was the children, with their prayers, who protected the inhabitants of Chamac. Once again, faith had saved them.

Helébora concludes her story with moist eyes, sensitive to each story she tells. For the spectators, she symbolizes the bond that unites them to a past full of mysteries that this young girl gradually unveils to them.

"And always remember that even in the hardest times there is hope."

The story has come to an end. Helébora looks around the auditorium from one end to the other looking for glances that would approve of her performance. Her face looks very attractive with those red cheeks, that smooth and lush complexion full of life. She proudly represents the inhabitants of the Andes. Those present, who were unaware of her history and background, let tears roll down their faces and applaud ecstatically. Outside the terral, a long line waits impatiently for Helébora, who is dismissed amid rumors and laughter from the audience.

Helébora's teachings and her sweet expression are captured in the heart of every visitor. She advances timidly to express her gratitude for entering the mysterious world of the Chancay dolls. The fervent applause continues.

"He speaks like an angel," murmured those present.

Spectators who attended the recital quickly spread the news.

"Go see the young girl standing in a vacant lot with a white flame. Her stories will move you."

At that very moment, very mysterious odors infiltrate the Kingdom of Darkness. The exhalations reach the palace of the anaconda like an aroma of ancient times. There is no room for doubt. Suddenly, inanimate images burst on the walls. Shapes of men, entire families and anguished children clamor for a little more time to live. As she leaves her palace, the anaconda witnesses winds, many winds, whipping through the Kingdom of Darkness.

"What strange breezes, where do they come from?" asks the anaconda.

"From the surface of the earth," replies the commander of his regiment.

"Something unusual is happening. This is unusual."

"Perhaps the forces of good are at work."

"Stop it!" she exclaims in anger."

Unable to wait a moment longer, she set off in irritation to the top of the mountains to consult the Oracle, for all that was happening was dangerous and needed an explanation. To know what is happening on earth. During its ascent, the anaconda sows devastation and, when it reaches the top of the mountain, it slips clandestinely until it finds itself in front of the Oracle.

"I have come here, Lord, to implore your mercy. I am troubled and tormented by doubts and forebodings that gnaw at my heart. Something strange is happening on earth and I need to know what. Please allow me to use my feline eyes a second time."

"Impossible, I can't lend them to you," answers the Oracle. I will go personally and tell you what my eyes have seen.

Plunging into the depths of the Andean winds, the Oracle descends to Picha. The fair is closing its doors until the next day, and only the organizers and a few artisans remain inside, cleaning and tidying up their kiosks. Helébora has just finished her story and proceeds to leave when a strong wind blows against her, making her stagger and lose her balance. The young girl falls face first to the ground.

At that very moment he hears his mother's anguished voice calling for help. The sidewalks are tangled with a thin film of dirty, stony earth covering the shop windows, kiosks and stands.

"Mom, where are you?" cries Helébora.

"Here, daughter! With the flames."

"Don't move, please. I'm coming."

Passing behind the kiosks, Helébora loses herself, wrist in hand, among the wide streets of the fair. From time to time she ducks to avoid being hit by an object or a stone that flies through the air.

After visiting the fair and seeing with his own eyes the unusual doll kiosk, the Oracle returns to the mountain to deliver a message: he speaks of protections and the end of this world due to the actions of mere mortals. The anaconda is devastated, she does not want to believe what she hears.

"Why? How? Do you still have the protections?"

"Yes, they are with me, but the ingenuity of mortals knows no bounds. Without having a single original on earth, the young girl has acquired a high degree of perfection in the dolls she has made. They are identical to the originals."

What the anaconda has just heard paralyzes her. An uneasiness takes hold of her, as if her blood were not circulating properly.

"Impossible! -she replied angrily. I refuse to believe it."

"I have no reason to lie to you. Many centuries ago the Andes succumbed under your yoke. But from now on you will witness the agony of your kingdom. You are no longer infallible and your nervousness will increase by the moment. Strong and reckless anaconda, get ready because a new era is coming to earth. An era that will mark the end of your existence."

"Why?"

"Because your weapons will be no match for love. You, anaconda, have become accustomed to using subterfuge to achieve your ends, but this time it will be impossible for you. Good will triumph on earth in spite of your wickedness."

At that precise moment, the anaconda feels a slight dizziness and closes its ears so as not to listen to any more fatalistic designs.

"Impossible!" she cries helplessly. Evil has cohabited with man for a long time, good will not be able to regain what it once lost. Pacha Rurac has disappeared; and with it, the protections.

"You are wrong, anaconda. The first seeds have already been planted in the soul of a young girl. She is the missing link, and sooner or later she will be the artificer of good."

Melted in grief, the beast feels vulnerable.

"I don't understand," he stammers. "At our last meeting you confirmed to me that mortals could not unravel the enigma of the dolls."

"I was wrong. I had underestimated the intelligence of mortals. The first stage is already underway," continues the Oracle, "and it is the descendant of Cumac who has initiated it."

"Cumac? That damn name rings a bell."

"She was the only survivor of the Pacha Rurac tragedy. Her descendant is protected. Now listen to me, good will gradually establish itself on Andean soil without you being able to prevent it. Any action on your part will only prolong your agony, but the paradox is that inaction will dig your grave."

"How to avoid it? Where to start?"

"The original protections are confined in the sacred temple. If they fall into the hands of mortals your end will be near. But don't worry, to achieve their purpose the distribution will have to be carried out by the descendant of Cumac. The Andean holding families will have to settle in their hometown. And only when these two requirements are fulfilled will the good settle definitively in the land. For the moment, nothing is lost."

But those words fail to calm the anaconda. What it is hearing is a declaration of war.

"Confining the dolls in the sacred temple? Oracle, we have to destroy them so that evil triumphs over its enemies!"

"Impossible, it is not in our power. Only mortals can do it."

Faced with such a devastating revelation, the anaconda has to be satisfied. In desperation, it implores the Oracle to allow it to send a few minions to the earth as observers. Seeing the animal's distress, the Oracle grants him this exceptional permission.

It has been a turbulent day, full of sorrows and unpleasant news. The anaconda returns to her kingdom alarmed and on the verge of losing her temper. Her anger leads her to utter piercing screams that shatter the walls.

Three henchmen approach.

"We have come to you, Excellency, to find out what is going on."

"I need you, my trusted men, to go to earth and bring me the direct descendant of Cumac. I want her alive," commands the anaconda, trying to contain her rage. "Find out to whom she has offered her dolls and destroy them. You will leave early tomorrow morning."

The Envoys
of the Anaconda

In the gloomy Kingdom of Darkness, the emissaries prepare for their mission. The great elm tree, guardian of the entrance to the kingdom of the anaconda, slowly climbs its heavy branches. Under the dawn of morning, the three emissaries set out to fulfill the beast's command. Ominous voices can be heard in the long tunnel between the earth and the Kingdom of Darkness: these are the most experienced and battle-hardened soldiers of the kingdom who are also preparing to ascend to the surface of the earth. The elm tree, faithful to the designs of its sovereign, extends its tangled roots to the depths of the earth to facilitate the ascent of the three men. As the emissaries climb the old roots, which crack at the slightest touch, they are hindered in their progress by the dust accumulated over the centuries. Disheartened after multiple falls and exhausted from so much effort, they return sweaty and hunched over to the palace.

There, they are witnesses and victims of the anaconda's angry outburst, which chases them away terrified so that they can try to climb again. After a tedious and exhausting process, with their thighs aching from so much pushing, the first of them manages to get to the surface.

A faint morning light greets the new arrivals, but the rest is a landscape of desolation and ruins. They are in what is left of Pacha Rurac. On the horizon they are presented with immense mountains under a pristine blue and clean sky that encourages them to move forward. Little by little, the scenery turns to the greenery of the plants and the colorful flowers. The three emissaries breathe in the scent as they gaze in awe at the magnitude and grandeur of the Andes. But they have a mission and they remind themselves not to be distracted for anything in the world.

They are disoriented as to where to go until they remember that some of their enemies were resting in the huaca of Pacha Rurac, erected by the Inca at the time of his death. The rest of the kingdom's bitter enemies are chained in the Hanan Pupu, the sacred mountain.

Invisible to the human eye, the three emissaries advance. They wear a grayish knee-length tunic, sandals, bracelets, anaconda tattoos on their chests, and rings and earrings on their ears and noses. They hide their gnawed faces with a large hood. Although no one can see them, they fail to go unnoticed, as the foul odor of their bodies can be perceived from miles away.

Ten roosters with colorful plumage crow out of tune to show their aversion to such individuals, and hundreds of dogs of the region bark as if possessed. The emissaries of the Kingdom of Darkness continue their mission amidst the whimpers and squeals of these disturbed animals. In their wake, the trees dry up and the leaves fall withered as a result of the putrid smell.

A cloud of dust accompanies the three emissaries, whose sinister moaning seems to emerge from the bowels of the earth until it reaches the most recondite regions of the Andes. Equipped with murderous weapons, the minions of the anaconda strike the ground again and again with rage until it opens up to reveal a deep wound. The terrible dust they create in their wake is dispersed and scattered everywhere.

They stop by the huaca of Pacha Rurac to make sure that the former inhabitants are still there, wrapped in their misery. There will be time to go to Hanan Pupu to see with their own eyes that the second group of unfortunate people continue to purge their punishment.

The invisible guards cross the moors and the ruins of Pacha Rurac; nature seems to step aside before the passage of the diabolical beings from another world. The black soul of the Kingdom of Darkness accompanies them.

In the huaca of Pacha Rurac, the twenty-five thousand souls that hold the alpaca wool ball with gold threads wake up uncomfortable because of the smell of carrion that circulates in the surroundings. That is not a good omen and the spirits find it hard to breathe in that stuffy air. It is a putrid smell that is familiar to them... A sudden fear of not completing their mission assails the community.

Panic spreads in the huaca as soon as the three guardians of the Kingdom of Darkness approach. The spirits hold hands to mitigate their anguish and pray in silence so as not to be discovered. In the distance they can hear the terrible cracking of the earth caused by the advance of those evil figures.

"We must warn Helébora," Ollantay commented, "I will go to the Patriarch of the sacred mountain, he will advise us how to do it."

"You can't go anywhere," Aucari argues. "We are facing the greatest danger we have ever faced. It would be a calamity if we were discovered. Unfortunately, there is nothing we can do but hide."

Hardly a few seconds have passed when footsteps are heard approaching the huaca where the spirits are sheltered. The women huddle frightened in a corner and the rest tune their ears to perceive the slightest noise that warns them of their terrible situation, so concentrated that they listen to the crackling of the dry leaves that a soft wind pulls from the trees. The footsteps intensify.

"They are the soldiers of the anaconda," Aucari whispers. "He has been on the alert since the dolls were made."

"I still think it is our duty to warn Helébora," insists Ollantay.

"Don't worry about her, she is the protector of the mountains," Aucari says quietly. The only thing we can do is to pray to our god that these soldiers find no sign of our presence."

The tension increases in the huaca as the enemies get closer. It is a real ordeal. Before long they could be discovered and in such a case the spirits would be sent to the Kingdom of Darkness for all eternity. Aucari observes their efforts to avoid moaning or making any noise that would give them away. He asks them for calm in those moments of danger. Kneeling in a corner, Ollantay desperately begs the Patriarch to come to his aid. Unfortunately, it is impossible for his most faithful friend to come to his aid. However, he does use an ancestral technique to communicate with Ollantay through a rock.

"Please, Patriarch, tell me what is going to happen."

"Ollantay, my intuition tells me that this encounter will bring great danger. Those henchmen of the anaconda will come to the fair. The protected of the mountains... could be affected."

Despite his distress, Ollantay thanks the Patriarch for his warning and approaches Aucari to share the information with him.

"I have never agreed with your celebrated Patriarch, but this time he is right. It is a matter of life or death. We must intervene as soon as these servants of the forces of evil move away from our huaca."

The emissaries of the anaconda are a few steps away from the huaca, and the spirits of Pacha Rurac are afraid of being discovered. Paralyzed by fear, they hold their breath. The henchmen scrutinize the hiding place, but sensing no vibration, they withdraw satisfied.

Serenity returns to the huaca as the emissaries of the anaconda walk away with hurried steps towards the Hanan Pupu, where they are greeted by the frozen faces of the spirits trapped there. The minions are again satisfied and continue on their way. This time to the Picha Fair. "Poor wretches," think the emissaries as they walk away from Hanan Pupu. "They must still endure their torment. They will give no trouble."

Their footsteps lead them to the outskirts of Picha, where the last visitors to the fair are strolling among the many attractions. The large number of attendees makes the emissaries' progress slow, but their resolve and intuitive ability increase as they approach the large wrought iron gate. Suddenly they stop before the first of the long row of kiosks, where a craftsman is busy arranging the pieces on display. Two of the emissaries of the anaconda watch while the third one squeezes the goldsmith's neck with his hands. The unfortunate man feels his throat tearing and his vocal cords are unable to emit any coherent sound. The poor man is unaware that he is pitted against evil. Waving his hands, he begs the unknown force to stop.

"If you want to free yourself from this torment," says an emissary, "tell us where is the woman who offers or talks about dolls.

"I don't know..." mumbles the craftsman without knowing who he is talking to. "Now I remember, yes... A girl offered a doll to a man."

"What man? -demands one of the invisible assailants."

The victim manages to free himself from those murderous hands for an instant, but in his attempt to escape he runs into another emissary, whose hand drags him back to the kiosk. The man is thrown to the ground unconscious. The emissaries exhibit unrelenting violence towards the craftsman, one of them throwing a bucket of water on him while several blows are inflicted on him. The three monsters give him a beating that the goldsmith will never forget. Invisible blows, but whose pain is very real. And the poor man reaches a point where the border between sanity and madness hangs by a thread.

"Am I going crazy?" he laments.

"Not at all, the pain you have felt is real. And if you don't cooperate, your life will be in danger."

"But... what can I tell you? I don't know anything... I don't even understand your questions."

The anaconda's envoys strike again.

"Memory, otherwise you can consider yourself a dead man."

"But who is speaking? I don't see anyone..."

"That's the least of it. For the second time, who did you give your doll to?"

"Hum..., I don't know."

The man receives a terrible punch in the belly and falls to the ground.

"Fool, refresh your memory!" shouts one of the emissaries. "You will dig your grave if you don't answer us now."

The artisan writhes in pain. Before his silence, he is dragged to a corner of the kiosk where he is the victim of another volley of blows, each one more violent.

"I swear I don't know anything," he pleads half-dead.

On the verge of fainting, the unfortunate man struggles to remember and respond to these threatening voices.

"Yes, I remember now. Helébora Rumi! That's the girl's name!"

"Keep going, don't stop!"

"She was Hatun Apu's assistant during the first days of the fair...."

"And then?"

"The goldsmith was forced to leave the fair. Apparently, a very important client needed him...."

"Did Hatun Apu get the first doll?"

"I don't think so, no... -Wait, I'm making a mistake. Yes... I remember now. Helébora gave it to Hatun Apu, but he left his kiosk very irritated. He even made a terrible threat to the girl."

"That Helébora Rumi... did she offer other dolls?"

"I wouldn't know."

"What about the visitors? Did they also have a doll?"

"I don't know either."

An emissary once again strikes his victim so violently that he falls to the ground. He then orders his two companions to destroy the kiosk before leaving. The craftsman, half unconscious, tries to get up as soon as the anaconda's henchmen leave, but falls to the ground again. Noting his poor condition, some of the men nearby volunteer to help him. Together they lift him up and place him in a chair. Someone offers him a glass of water to calm him down.

"What happened here?"

"I-I don't know..."

"Are you all right? Are you all right?"

"No! I need to get out of here..."

Immediately, the artisan takes his poncho and disappears into the crowd without adding a single word. He then left the fair in panic. The visitors go in search of one of the organizers to tell them what has happened. The organizers were surprised by the strangeness of the situation and tried to reassure the visitors.

"Thank you for informing us of this incident. We will take care of it."

Visitors to the fair still walk away intrigued.

Meanwhile, the servants of darkness, satisfied with the information gathered, decide to move on to the next stage and smear their face, arms and chest with a paprika-based paste in accordance with a rite of the Kingdom of Darkness before proceeding to attack their next victim: Helébora.

They move forward without hesitation, giving pushes and slaps to those who cross their path. Suddenly the emissaries realize that the crowd that circulates through the streets of the fair is heading en masse towards the back, where the protected of the mountains is located. Some passers-by turn away when they notice the terrible smell emanating from the anaconda's envoys. On their way to Helébora's kiosk, the three henchmen encounter a strange creature. It is an old man with a long scruffy beard who has guessed their intentions and approaches them with feeble steps to convey a message. He can see the emissaries.

"They won't be able to finish Helébora today. Not while she is under powerful protection. Your expedition is doomed to failure, servants of evil."

"Shut up, you wretch!" one of the envoys snaps. "Who are you?"

"I can be very useful," says the old man with a mysterious air. I know many things that might interest you."

"Out of our way!" another emissary rudely replies, "Look! You can barely walk and you pretend to give us advice."

"Who is this insolent man who dares to stand in our way?" asks another.

The evil of the emissaries knows no bounds. Without thinking twice, one of them thrusts his spear into the old man's foot. The poor man falls to the ground complaining of a sharp pain; strangely the discomfort spreads to the other foot although he has not received any wound. Then the evil begins to ascend in his knees. The terrified old man takes off his poncho and his wild eyes discover a horrible sight: long, thick hair covers his legs down to his knees, and black goat hooves replace his feet. For a moment he thinks he is losing his mind. The old man, in a broken voice, begs the emissaries to put an end to the torment.

"This is the fruit of your insolence," one of them replied with a sardonic laugh. "Get out, don't cross our path anymore."

The other two laugh and cover him with insults and threats. Limping and crying, the old man manages to get away from the eyes of the crowd. He is suffering, but the shame of humiliation is more intense. He hurries to hide this repellent transformation from the eyes of others. The mutation is not only physical, but a spell operates within him: his mind and soul have also been corrupted by a relentless poison that is turning the brave old man into a mean and evil being. Without knowing it yet, he has just changed sides and will soon be at the service of the anaconda as one of its best servants.

For the guardians, the incident is already forgotten and they continue with their mission. They venture with rapid pace to the place where Helébora is found. The smells of decomposition begin to disturb the visitors gathered there, affecting their noses and throats. The air becomes unbearable and no one can identify the source of the stench. The infamous emissaries become excited as they feel they are approaching their goal. Finally, they are very close to their prey, the last descendant of Cumac. Their plan is simple and brutal: drag her by her wrists to the Kingdom of Darkness where her master has a deadly spell in store for her.

Shortly before the arrival of the anaconda's emissaries, Fortunata leaves the wasteland where Helébora is with one of the llamas to feed the second one. Finding no grass for her to chew on, she goes to ask the organizers for information.

Unaware of the danger she is in, Helébora begins a new story for her audience in the terral. In order to illustrate it better, she places a large brightly colored blanket at the feet of the white flame and prepares the Inca vessels containing the dolls for distribution when the story is finished. The emissaries of the anaconda witness these minimal movements, and impatient, but self-confident, they advance towards the first benches.

"Come on, let's get this over with!"

They advance towards the storyteller armed with their formidable spears. Helébora directs her gaze towards the audience without noticing anything peculiar when, suddenly, an icy and putrid breeze rushes over her face and body. It is like an echo from beyond the grave followed by a foul-smelling dust that rises up with a single purpose: to create chaos and make it easier for evil to triumph over the earth.

"Go!" ordered one of the emissaries. "Catch her without hurting her, we must take her alive to the Kingdom of Darkness."

Helébora hears these voices from beyond the grave, followed by energetic footsteps. Then she sees the terrifyingly fresh footprints on the earthen floor and thinks she hears a strange conversation.

A fear takes hold of the poor craftswoman, who trembles from head to toe. Instinctively, her eyes scan the surroundings without seeing any threat. The crowd is calm; however, she feels that she is being watched. And she is not mistaken.

In a few seconds, the anaconda's henchmen surround her, under the slogan of not letting her escape. And that is how evil slips out of the shadows and stands in front of her. Powerful hands grab Helébora, forcibly dragging her across the earth. Completely dazed, she is unable to see her assailants. "What to do in the face of such terrible circumstances?" asks Helébora.

She has no words to describe what she is experiencing. The chilling spiral of violence overwhelms her, everything is so fleeting that Helébora can barely put up any resistance. But she fights, she does not let herself be dragged down, fearing that this is the end of her existence. Everything is beyond her understanding, for nothing in this maddening situation seems to have an explanation. The impossible happens in full view of all those present. They wonder why Helébora does not conclude the story while fear is drawn on the faces of those who watch her struggle to free herself from her oppressors. It is as if the girl had been gripped with strong pincers, making it impossible for her to escape. Helébora hits the ground with her violent movements, shakes her arms and cries with impotence. The audience leaves the room in terror.

Helébora's punishment is not due to any betrayal, lie or deceit. It is due to her daring to spread what she longed for: the protections of the Chancay dolls. On previous occasions, Helébora has shown great ingenuity in the face of adversity. But now she is short of ideas.

"Who are you?" she asks, perturbed, to the invisible force that imprisons her. What do you want from me?"

The emissaries of the anaconda do not respond, pretending not to hear her. These invisible beings only have in mind to present their prisoner to their master. Helébora looks around her for the last time: the lively fair, the Andes, the life on earth...

"Help! Help!" she cries helplessly.

"Save your saliva," says an invisible being, "and prepare to live your worst torment."

With her eyes full of tears, Helébora wonders what sin she has committed to receive such a punishment. She turns her head to look at the flames, the Inca vases with the dolls inside and her mother, a little further away. It may be the last thing she sees of her life.

In the huaca of Pacha Rurac, not far from the fair, the news of the abduction causes panic.

"The time for questioning is over, textile master! It's your turn and this time there's no room for mistakes!"

Uneasy and lost in thought, the textile master feels the pressure of the situation. He is facing a great test and much is expected of him, but he is not sure how to meet the challenge. The likelihood of success is slim and, plagued by dark thoughts, he questions his own experience. At times it comes to his mind to communicate to others that he is not the right person for the task, but it is too late. They have already sacrificed much to recover from the ball of alpaca wool with gold strands and cannot back down. Even worse, he is unable to look his curaca in the face. "If I make a mistake, will I find peace? It won't work, it won't work..." he repeats to himself a thousand times with sadness. Besides, how can he free Helébora from danger?

The members of the community silently follow the movements of the one in whom they have placed all their hopes. The master of textiles tries to remain calm and does not allow others to notice the disorder in which he lives. He takes a deep breath and entrusts himself to his father's soul for courage. In the absence of instructions, he says a long and fervent prayer before letting himself be guided by his own intuition. Her father bequeathed her an ancient loom, handed down by her ancestors.

"Use it in times of distress," his father told him when he gave him the treasure. Then its powers will carry you far and high. Far and high...

Undoubtedly these were the key words to reinforce the textile master's confidence. Without delay and full of optimism, he lifts the ball of alpaca wool with golden threads to the sky and begins his delicate work. First, he fixes his father's loom to the ground, then inserts the thread of the wool ball into the needle of his work tool and turns the filament towards the sky.

The fear of the community increases as the ball of alpaca wool with gold strands rises into the air, none of them know how to free the wrists from the Oracle's chambers and they are not convinced that this fragile thread can give them back their old protections, it seems unable to support the weight of the wrists in their descent to earth. But, to everyone's surprise, the ball of wool seems to perform its function with disconcerting ease and precision.

However, one problem remains: what will happen if the Oracle discovers the woolen thread? Would all be lost? To assuage the concerns of the other spirits, the textile master suppresses that threat by conjuring a spell that renders the thread invisible.

The prodigy continues to wander through the sacred temple of the Oracle, slipping by stealthily. Finally, the needle finds the captive dolls, huddled for centuries in a dark corner. Taking control of the situation, the magical tip of the needle binds the hands of two dolls in a knot and repeats the process with the others. The Oracle, meditating in the prayer room, does not notice the fateful outcome. The corridors of the temple are deserted, with no one to prevent the dolls from escaping and, little by little, they descend until they are hidden by the clouds.

Aucari and her spirits wait impatiently for a joyful outcome, with their eyes raised to the sky, scrutinizing it with the longing to see their precious Chancay dolls again.

But the huaca panics when the textile master depressedly announces that, after completing some calculations, the thread requires an external force to find its way back. Otherwise it will remain suspended in the air or be lost forever in the clouds.

"What are we going to do? -they ask in dismay."

The situation is complicated, especially now that twilight is setting in, and speculation about the future is rife; some tragic, some extravagant and very few optimistic.

"The thread has been cut," some say, somewhat depressed.

"No, it's tangled in a rock or in some trees," say others.

"Or perhaps stuck in the necks of the dolls."

The threat of being discovered is latent.

"Have we committed a vile daring?"

"Will we be punished for it?"

Sorrowful, his eyes remain fixed on the sky. Despite the dire premonitions, the textile master remains focused on his work, directing the magic thread with the utmost rigor. But in the face of the agonizing expectation, Aucari's patience is exhausted and the priest considers that the situation is getting out of hand. His decision is to give up.

"It's all over," says Aucari.

"Keep calm, please," Ollantay asks. "We all know that the unknown can terrify even the bravest, but let the textile master finish his work. I am sure he will bring us to a good end."

Consternation descends upon the community, but it does not last long. One of the spirits, whose gaze has been fixed on the sky, catches a sort of colorful comet that catches his attention. When it descends a little further, he can clearly see that it is a battalion of brightly colored cloth dolls. For the first time in a long time, Aucari regains her lost optimism and hope. The dolls, the authentic Chancay dolls that have protected her community in the past, descend from the sky tied with the famous alpaca wool thread with gold strands.

"We are saved!" exclaims Aucari, unable to contain her joy. "What a relief!"

They have won the first battle against their greatest enemy. The joy is indescribable. Quickly, groups are formed, dancing, jumping, jumping, shouting and even hugging and kissing each other. The happiness is absolute. However, despite being enraptured by the dolls falling from the sky, they remember that their work is not yet finished. They must hurry to recover the dolls that they themselves have made with the help of Helébora. The orders of the curaca are clear: to go directly to the earth and extract them from the Inca vases.

Meanwhile, hope is still suspended in the air. Cleverly, the ingenious spirits redirect the wool fiber into Inca vases. Mission accomplished. Farewell, torments, anxieties and anxieties. From now on, good will spread in the Andean territory so as not to be expelled again.

At the Picha Fair, Fortunata hears the anguished cries of her daughter in danger. Immediately, she abandons what she is doing and runs to meet her. Arriving at the place where the screams came from, she witnesses a surreal sight: Helébora struggles as if trying to free herself from someone Fortunata cannot see. The scene is horrifying, and the mother cannot understand that her daughter is being kidnapped.

Helébora fights with all her strength, with blows, slaps and scratches. It is terrible to see her in this state. Fearing the worst, her mother tries in vain to grab her by the arm, but in the struggle she realizes that the invisible force that imprisons her daughter is very powerful. Fortunata clears her doubts.

"Oh, no! Evil forces have come for you, my daughter," exclaims the mother, "I won't let them take you!"

"It's no use, Mom. They are too strong. Go away and leave me alone with my sentence."

Her mother runs stumbling after her, far from disheartened.

"Courage, my daughter!"

Helébora is dragged out of the fair with her hands tied. She only wanted to offer the Chancay dolls that had once protected the Andean people. So what is going on? It seems inconceivable to her that her effort to recover Inca traditions has turned into a heap of misfortune. No doubt the end is near.

But all is not lost, for fate has a pleasant surprise in store for Helébora, and it manifests itself in an unexpected way. Fine particles, barely visible to the human eye, spread across the sky, tracing an unusual path that leaves a trail of dark spots. Later they appear as blurry colored silhouettes until, finally, they reveal themselves as dolls.

They descend towards Helébora.

A spring of golden light rushes against the ground and advances in two directions. The first one goes to Cuchimilcos; the second one, the most imposing and majestic, brings tumultuous winds that head towards the Inca vases, where the brave spirits commanded by Aucari remove the Chancay dolls made by Helébora to leave free space for the originals.

The unusual has flooded Helébora's life. A multitude of visitors to the fair raise their eyes to the sky to contemplate this magical apparition. The authentic dolls take their place inside the Inca vases. From there they open their eyes to discharge their power, depriving evil of all action.

The miracle is reborn.

Flashes of happiness flood the exhibition. It is as if a spark of goodness spreads through the world, with such luminosity that the envoys of the anaconda, accustomed to darkness, are blinded. Something is transformed in them. Love beats in their hearts as their strength diminishes, weakening to the point where no trace of their belligerence and evil intentions remains. After a few moments, the stunned minions languish, not knowing what to do, until they finally release their hold on Helebora and return to the Realm of Darkness.

Once there, they present themselves in the palace of the anaconda, where they kneel panting before their sovereign. They recount their expedition in detail, but omit the incident with Helebora. Now erased from their memory.

"The confession of a man we beat confirms that Hatun Apu, the famous goldsmith descended from the Incas, stayed with the storyteller during the first days of the fair and then left."

"Did that man acquire a doll?"

"According to this individual's confession, he received a doll as a gift."

"That Hatun Apu, son of the Incas, will never set foot in the Andes again. From today, wherever you are and whatever you do, my dear Hatun Apu, your life will be a disaster," swears the anaconda. "And the girl, where is the descendant of Cumac?"

"We have not found her."

The beast is seized with rage when he hears that his envoys have failed in their mission, he has only heard a banal narrative that offers no clue as to the whereabouts of Cumac's lineage. In order not to show weakness before his subjects, the beast expels his three emissaries from the Kingdom of Darkness.

In Picha everything is back to normal. Helébora finds herself in the main artery of the fair, accompanied by her mother and the Inca vases, watching as the avenues and empty kiosks are once again flooded with a crowd milling around, anxious not to miss the tale of another legend. The crowd squeezes into the seats to listen to Helébora and the less fortunate settle as best they can at the back. A beautiful story awaits them that will keep their illusion alive for the rest of their days.

Helébora describes silent gestures with her hands as she walks around the auditorium with a deep gaze. As if she were in a cathedral, the girl prepares to take communion with her followers.

This legend has its origin in pre-Inca times," he announces with a powerful voice, "in the ancient Puru Puru Puru, annexed to the majestic empire of Tahuantinsuyo. Prosperity reigned in their domains. Its fertile lands provided them with the healthiest crops in the region, its very rich mountains provided invaluable treasures, its lakes bathed a large part of the territory and the solid constructions of its city offered security to its inhabitants. Nothing portended any misfortune. Thanks to the strength and courage of its troops, Puru Puru was highly respected in its time. The agility and dexterity of its soldiers was recognized throughout the region. At the age of fifteen, Puru Puru's young men were recruited into his army for a period of five years. The lord of those lands, already old and exhausted, counted as direct descendants his daughter Dulchicea, the most beautiful creature of the Andean territory. Seeing that his days were numbered, he proclaimed to the four winds that the time had come for his daughter to marry. To this end, he invited all the princes and nobles of the neighboring towns to court Dulchicea. The young men, worthy representatives of their respective tribes, paraded before the governor and his young daughter laden with treasures, ointments, perfumes, alpaca capes and vicuña garments. All without exception succumbed to the almost unreal beauty of the young girl. However, Dulchicea, whose heart did not sigh for any of the suitors, continued with her desire to remain a virgin.

Prince Curi, chief of a savage tribe and one of the greatest and most fearsome rulers, heard about the beauty of that princess. Unlike his adversaries, he did not show up with huge loads of jewels and precious objects. Lacking scruples, Curi would use a very particular strategy: to subdue the people of Puru Puru by force. "If Dulchicea is not mine by love, it will be mine by arms", he swore.

The time came for the festivities of the Sun God. The people, in recognition of the abundance after the last rains, fervently thanked their only god. The father of Dulchicea decreed a whole week of celebrations and festivities. The entire population went into the various streets and squares of the city, Puru Puru was so lively that only joy was breathed. The festivities were extended during the night, when, accompanied by renowned musicians and dancers, crushing coca and drinking chicha de jora, the people gave themselves completely to the celebration. However, during the last day of celebrations some strange events took place in the city. The night before, the dogs had barked irrationally and an owl with eyes from beyond the grave had landed on the roof of Princess Dulchicea's chambers. "An owl!" exclaimed the princess in fright. It is a bad omen. Get it out of here at once." Returning to her bed-chamber, she discovered that the flowers that had just been picked were wilting rapidly; the dried petals were falling one by one, and the yellowish stems remained stiff. The princess, like most of the inhabitants of Puru Puru, believed in warnings and premonitory signs. Frightened, she ordered her servants to go in search of a shaman who could interpret what had happened. At that very moment, an unknown woman demanded to speak with Dulchicea. "I bring a very important message for the princess. You must listen to me. The sovereign's daughter, a little confused, went out to meet the woman whose appearance revealed that she was not from Puru Puru. Listen to me well, princess, since what I am going to tell you is very important. Much suffering will befall you. My beautiful girl, a mysterious paradox is brewing on the horizon. Your incalculable beauty, which is the pride of your people, will also be the cause of their destruction". Hearing such a prediction, Dulchicea ran out of her rooms to beg her father to send a troop to protect the outskirts of the city. The soldiers were summoned, but, dulled by the effects of the alcohol consumed during the festivities, their gestures were incoherent and uncertain. The foreboding winds blew convulsively, shaking some of the inhabitants. A troubled sky was slowly advancing, completely covering Puru Puru. Somewhere on the outskirts of the city, the order to attack was given.

Coming from no one knew where, a regiment of soldiers entered the city of Puru Puru, which little by little was taken over by invaders. The half-drunken people stood in the main square looking curiously at the deployment of foreign troops. These were Prince Curi's best warriors, but they remained inactive, as mere silent observers. However, those unfriendly painted faces conveyed a smell of carrion that permeated the tense atmosphere. After that pause, Curi's gesture was enough for his horde to attack the surprised inhabitants of Puru Puru.

Dulchicea was in the litter carrying her retinue, trying to warn her people when she encountered the surprise attack. The princess immediately ordered her retinue to conduct her to the safety of their quarters. Prince Curi, at the head of his troop, advanced towards the central square giving orders to kill every living thing. Curi's men scattered through the narrow streets of the city, hurling flaming arrows at buildings, spreading fires. The entire city burned. The fire spread rapidly and the black plumes of smoke and the piercing cries of death bore witness to the horrendous massacres. The inhabitants, weak from the effects of the chicha, ran desperately in search of shelter from their perfidious aggressors. A handful of Puru Puru soldiers fought to defend their own; however, they were quickly liquidated.

Arriving at her rooms, the terrified princess rushed to grab her Chancay doll. Her elderly father followed her. Prince Curi, upon seeing her flee, threw himself after her, massacring Dulchicea's faithful entourage without them being able to resist. When he saw the disgusting intentions of that man, the governor of Puru Puru tried to protect his daughter, but was viciously stabbed in the presence of the princess. Feeling himself master of his prey, Prince Curi advanced towards her full of arrogance and pride. Grabbing her by the waist, he carried her on his shoulders and proudly displayed his prey. Dulchicea gave in to such cruelty and her heart aspired to nothing and, without shedding a single tear, she uttered these words: "The deepest pain has been to see with my own eyes the death of my father and mine. My life no longer has any meaning. Before those arms that imprisoned her soft skin, Dulchicea was driven away from her city of narrow streets and green hope, now tinged with a terrifying black. The princess clung desperately to her wrist, pressing herself against it, and with an almost insane instinct she asked the firmament to help her overcome her misfortune. In the blink of an eye the princess was reduced to the rank of a mere woman, silently enduring the outrages and tortures inflicted on her kingdom and its inhabitants. Submerged by a deep sadness, Dulchicea withdrew into herself, allowing herself to be carried away by the waves of suffering.

After sowing devastation in Puru Puru, Prince Curi and his army advanced towards the sacred valley of Huacu, located on the edge of the Amazon jungle, where Dulchicea was confined in a cell built on top of a fortress on the edge of a precipice. Thus, any attempt to escape was in vain. Still dismayed by the tragedy, Dulchicea wept bitterly imploring her doll. "Can you tell me why the village of Puru Puru has been completely destroyed? Why didn't you do anything to prevent it? I strive to live, but nothing holds me back." The limp doll did not respond to his lamentations.

Prince Curi was overwhelmed by Dulchicea's marvelous beauty and ordered a grandiose display for the preparations of their union, ordering the most ostentatious party to be organized. Dulchicea received frequent visits from women who took her measurements: her body for the dress, her head for a crown and her feet for the sandals. The princess surrendered to these so-called attentions.

During her captivity, Dulchicea let herself be overcome by disappointment. Neither her confinement nor her nuptials mattered to her, for her will to live was broken. Every night she implored her doll to work the miracle of turning her into a bird to escape from that fierce torment. One dark starry night, after so many prayers, her doll's eyes lit up with an intensity similar to that of the sun. Her cell was completely illuminated and a condor appeared. The bird approached softly and called to the princess tenderly. "Dulchicea, Dulchicea! Wake up, I've come to help you escape," said the condor. "Escape to where? And who are you?" replied the princess in surprise. "I have come to your rescue through your doll and your prayers. I am aware of your misfortunes and the destruction of your people. But fate has another life in store for you. From today, you will be the dove that will bring hope to the oppressed peoples of the Andes. Come on, come with me. Come with me. Dulchicea, who saw that her life was meaningless in that fortress, begged the condor: "Please, take me with you. Away from here. Away from this land. I need to forget. And, after clinging tightly to the condor's feet, whose pleasant warmth the princess felt, the bird spread its wings and flew away with the princess.

In a matter of seconds, Dulchicea became urpi-cha-lla-y.[11] She followed the condor as it showed her the oppressed peoples of the Andes. He deposited her on top of the sacred mountain of Vilcanota, where she was enveloped by an unusual clarity and a voice from the bowels of the mountain: "Urpi-cha-lla-y, light of the Andean peoples. Urpi-cha-lla-y, light of the oppressed

---

[11] 'Dove' in Quechua.

peoples". From that moment on, Dulchicea was blessed by the god of the mountains. Intoxicated by this divine mandate, the princess's face shone with happiness as she found her reason for being, the peace and tranquility she thought she had lost. Her body faded away until it became a light that dispersed among the needy peoples. Dulchicea realized that her future had a meaning: she could enlighten every oppressed soul in the Andes.

The next morning, Curi was informed of the disappearance of the princess. The fortress was very solid and remote, so he thought it was impossible that she had escaped. Arriving at his cell, the prince confirmed her absence and noticed the Chancay doll abandoned in a corner. As he picked it up, the shadow of his wickedness was projected on the face of that rag doll. Curi watched in bewilderment as an almost hurtful smile was drawn on its jute face. The prince did not believe that such a fragile and delicate young woman would be capable of running away in such an inhospitable and rugged place. Before long, he realized that his bloodthirsty and destructive methods had not yielded the results he had hoped for: the princess of Puru Puru Puru had not bowed to his vile torment. Helpless, Curi realized that he held in his hands a doll whose mysterious eyes penetrated his being. An intense cold seized him. His mind screamed at him to run away and leave the doll, but his heart begged him to stay there, holding it. Perhaps that rag figure would reveal to him the location of the lost princess.

The cowardly massacre of the Puru Puru people tormented him. Regrets, sorrows and sadness deformed his sick mind and, little by little, took hold of him. Curi enveloped his soul with gloomy forebodings. Some days later, his trusted soldiers took him out of Dulchicea's room and transported him to his quarters, where he remained inert for weeks. Upon learning of what happened, his relatives, stung by the ambition of power and the desire to take possession of the kingdom of Curi, unleashed the bloodiest fratricidal wars in the region, thus destroying the entire dynasty of the destroyers of Puru Puru.

Helébora stands up at the conclusion.

"This story carries two messages," he tells his audience. "The first is that he who sows the winds reaps the storms; the second is that our lives are in constant mutation. Sometimes we are at the top and sometimes on the lowest rungs, but no one is master of his or her destiny. However, in the ups and downs you will always find a little light that will tell you, 'Hold on to life, there is still hope.'"

In those magical moments, Helébora's voice, gestures and gaze seem to harbor a double meaning. They are very tender moments. Moments of calm and enchantment. The audience did not know this story and its origin, but the girl has narrated it with such emotion that some tears are shed. Then comes the explosion of applause. And soon after, the distribution of Chancay dolls begins, the benefits of which start as soon as they fall into the hands of an owner. With each family that receives a doll, its protection spreads throughout the Andean territory.

In a short time, waves of happiness spread through the air while, underground, a real cataclysm devastated the Kingdom of Darkness, whose darkness lost ground. This is how good establishes itself everywhere and spreads rapidly through the kingdom of the anaconda.

In the town of Cuchimilcos, Don Gumersindo has been restless and anxious since the departure of Helébora and Fortunata, as he sees it difficult for the two women to return from the fair. Time moves inexorably forward and he still has no news of them... In this delirious anguish, he hears a dull rumor, like a gust of wind that blows through the town. Don Gumersindo rises abruptly to the door and opens it wide. Trying to identify the origin of this noise, he observes in the sky hundreds of dolls descending on Cuchimilcos. One by one, they enter each home.

It is a miracle, a true miracle of the Andes! One of these dolls is placed on his table, giving great serenity to the wise man. This marvelous event speaks for itself and Don Gumersindo, who knows the secrets, is convinced that Helébora has succeeded in spite of the obstacles encountered. Action after action, she has led the Andes to their liberation.

A new wind is blowing in the Andean territory.

In the prisons of the Kingdom of Darkness, similar incidents plague the terrified guards, who wonder what is going on. Chacta, chained in his cell, offers them the answer:

"Didn't you understand, anaconda? Your time is up: the good is settling in."

The atmosphere changes completely when a sense of peace begins to circulate in the air. The beast orders his numerous patrols to retaliate against this atrocious threat. Unfortunately, his army is hampered. Paralyzed.

Powerless in the face of these facts, the anaconda slips on the ground without imagining that a transformation is gradually taking place in her. An intense cold in the air orders her to leave her kingdom, but her heart cries out to her that she must remain there, where she is most needed. Gradually, her body stops obeying her and she becomes numb from the cold. Only her brain seems immune, as her thoughts fly back to that horrible day when, blinded by a thirst for revenge and power, she exterminated the people of Pacha Rurac. These images of horror and destruction occupy his mind. Petrified, he begs forgiveness for all the harm he has caused.

But it is too late. There is nothing left to do: he is now a prisoner of his body and his sin.

Days later, her disoriented soldiers decide to take her out of her palace and expose her at the border of the kingdom.

In Picha, a roar of applause greeted Helébora. She has triumphed.

"It is the prophecy of the Andes," whispers Fortunata to her daughter, "the one that Don Gumersindo foretold me before your birth: "Behind a crystal wall and its golden-eyed door, the flower that will free the Andes from the forces of evil will receive the life of Lady Fortuna".

Looking up to heaven, the mother thanks God with all her heart for allowing this precious human being to be born.

This is how the first steps towards good are taken, with a girl who becomes the icon of an entire people, the incarnation of the freedom of her beloved Andean territory.